The Unexpected Cost of Love

The Unexpected Cost of Love
By Mark T. Sneed

ISBN: 978-1-7366698-8-4

Table of Contents

DEDICATION

To my mother, family and friends who continue to inspire, encourage and challenge me to be a better person.

THANK YOU

To all the unsung dreamers, visionaries, believers, questioners, who possess the faith and belief in their convictions despite what others say or attempt to dismiss as impossible. Thank you for attempting to hold onto your beliefs, dreams and ideas not to spite but to enlighten those of what a different perspective and trust can manifest in the face of seemingly insurmountable odds.

The Unexpected Cost of Love

The Unexpected Cost of Love
By Mark T. Sneed

Chapter 1.

Kyla Hudson was unquestionably the hottest and brightest girl at Foothill High School. She was rich. She was beautiful. She was this desert beauty who had this perfect life. Every boy had tried to go out with Kyla Hudson, but all had failed to hold her interest. More importantly, every boy had failed to impress Kyla's father, Kyle Hudson, the most successful Black realtor in Las Vegas. Failing to impress Kyle Hudson spelt a short-lived relationship with his only daughter.

I knew all this because everyone told me once they learned that she and I had just begun going out after I helped her with some math. Well, she helped me. Two weeks into our relationship things got really interesting. I felt like I was in some action movie when Kyla decided to spice up her life, just a little and zig rather than zag for a day.

I thought it was kind of flattering. I mean, here I was just Cam Weaver, a nobody, compared to Kyla, and she had picked me to bend her dad's rules with. Every day she was picked up by her assigned guards and whisked back up to her mansion.

The first time I had gone to the Hudson mansion was nerve wracking.

I recalled that first night and all the build up to it.

Saturday came and I tried to keep it casual. I wasn't going to let Kyla's paranoia and family issues throw me. I had breakfast with my mom. I lazed around the house and tried to not think about the dinner coming.

After breakfast I texted Kyla.

GM Ky. Hope you're good.

Saturday was the day that my mom and I went to garage sales. Most garage sales began early, well early for Saturday mornings. My mom and I were out of the house by nine and usually home by no later than two o'clock in the afternoon.

"Mom, you know, I have a thing tonight? Right?"

"I know," my mother said.

On a good Saturday we would hit at least a dozen garage, estate and yard sales, looking for whatever my mother was looking for. I think that she just loved bartering and talking sellers down to reasonable prices she imagined in her head. When we walked into a garage sale my mother was always looking for something that caught her eye. When she found it, she was always aloof and uncertain if the thing she wanted was authentic and worth it. She asked ten questions and if the answers were correct, she then walked them down on the final price.

It was like a retail movie. All the junk of others. All these outlandish prices and expectations of someone feeling that their junk had some value. It was a snore fest for me. I always was bored and looking for the odd valuable, but never really that interested.

That Saturday we hit just under ten garage and yard sales before heading to an estate sale.

Kyla texted me around noon.

Just checking in. You okay?

I'm good.

You still coming to dinner?

Yeah.

Okay. See you at seven.

Got it.

Wes texted me around one.

You ready?

Ready?

To meet the parents?

Ha.

Think it might be more like Godfather.

You are too funny.

If her dad makes you an offer, don't refuse.

Ha.

The estate sale was large and expansive, but my mother was a very specific in her hunt. Of course, before returning home, we had to stop by Urban Crawfish Station. We had lunch there before heading home.

My mom had me do a few things around the house. I had to take out the garbage. She asked me to move the couch in the living room. I was also supposed to replace a burned-out light in her bathroom.

Lyle texted me.

Cam. Do me a favor. Get pictures.

Of what?

The house. Heard it was a mini mansion.

I'll think about it.

Thanks. Also get a picture of the pool.

Justice texted me around three.

What you up to?

Nothing.

Just checking in.

Cool.

All right. Thinking of going to the movies later.

Not available.

Oh, yeah. Well, good luck.

Thanks.

I wanted to ask about the movie they were going to, but I chose not to concern myself with that. Instead, I focused on preparing for the dinner a few hours away.

Instead, after unloading the treasures my mom had found at the estate sale, I went to dress. My mom sat at her prized café table and pulled out her notebook and all the scraps of paper that she had gathered for her dream antique shop.

I left my mom in the kitchen and headed to my bedroom. Once there I decided to wash up and then looked for a T-shirt to wear. I found a T-shirt and opted out of the T-shirt and jeans look. I put on one of my collared shirts and found a belt. I was still wearing my jeans and sneakers. I did change my jeans, since they were dirty and dusty from rummaging. Dressed in a collared shirt, jeans and sneakers I decided I had to be myself even if I was meeting Kyla's parents.

Coming out of my bedroom my mom was still sitting at the café table.

She looked at me and scanned me from head to toe silently. She smiled but did not say a word.

"Remember I am going to dinner?"

She took my words in. She nodded. She did not say anything.

"Do you remember?"

She took my new interest in stride. My mom seemed to understand. It was inevitable.

I didn't know what I expected but my mother sitting at the café table in the kitchen looking at me without a word was not it. I had never had a girlfriend before. I didn't know how the whole thing worked. I had seen boys with girlfriends in school and they were ultra-protective. I never wanted to be like that. My mom was incredibly quiet when it came to her relations, if she had any. So, I relied on Wes, Lyle and Justice and sometimes Tommy and X, from the neighborhood for help.

Honestly, they were little to no help. They reminded me of those guys in church who talked about stopping coming to church, but every Sunday they were there. I needed to talk to someone who had experience, but I just didn't know who to listen to.

I supposed that I never imagined having a girlfriend and more importantly, never imagined it would be Kyla Hudson. My life, because of my math teacher, had suddenly taken an unexpected turn and development.

"Cam? Are you okay?"

I took a breath.

"Yeah," I said. "I'm fine."

I smiled at my mother and realized that for all she did as my mom, the provider, my nurse when I was sick and a host of other things, this was now on me. If I succeeded or failed with Kyla, then it would be on me. I wanted advice. I needed advice, but sometimes, a few times, in life, you have to walk through doors all alone.

My mother smiled in her uniquely mom fashion. The corner of her mouth curled and there was a slight twinkle in her eye before she spoke.

"You ready?"

"I think so," I said.

"Well, you look nice," my mother said with a small smile.

"I just want things to work out," I said.

My mother did not respond. She just sat at her café table playing with the papers on the tabletop.

I looked at her curiously. In the back of my mind, I imagined she had forgotten I was heading to dinner with Kyla and her family.

"You know I'm going to dinner with Kyla and her family? Right?"

"I do," she said.

"Well, what do you think of it?"

"Well, I think it's sweet. I think I said that before," she said. She looked up and studied me. "I just don't know why you telling me?"

Why am I telling you? You are my mother, I wanted to say. You are the person I talk to about everything, I thought.

I looked at my mom and shook my head.

"I just figured if I came up missing you might want to know who to blame," I said with a big smile.

"So, tell me again, who this is?"

"It's the Hudson's," I said again to my mother as she sat looking at me like I had just grown an extra finger or arm. "You know them. Everyone knows them."

"The real estate people?"

"Yeah, that's them," I said.

"Okay," my mother said with a nod of her head. "Here's my advice. I don't have too much, but here goes. One, say, "Yes sir and No sir." The rich love that. Say, "Yes ma'am and No ma'am" when you get a chance. When they talk to you don't act any different than you would if you were talking to me. If you like this girl then you have to be the person she knows. Don't try to impress them. They may have a little more than us, but that doesn't mean they are better. It just means they got a lucky break somewhere." My mother paused, thinking. "When it comes to eating use your knife and fork. If it's chicken, you can eat that with your hand." My mother closed her eyes and bit her bottom lip, thinking. "I think that is all the advice I got for you Cam. Just be yourself and be polite and enjoy your chance to meet the family. If you and this girl hit it off, then you might have to bring her over to meet me."

"Yeah, okay," I said with a laugh. I checked my phone for the time. I walked to the café table and hugged my mom before I left the house and headed to see Kyla.

When I drove up to Kyla's home, I knew that the family was going to try and frighten me off with all their money and power. I pulled up to the front gate and waited as the gate swung open and allowed my Volkswagen Jetta to enter the circular drive where there were half a dozen cars parked already that could have bought three or four homes if I cashed them in. I parked behind a convertible Bentley four door sedan and a Porsche Cayenne. As I climbed out of my car, I found myself confronted by two men dressed in dark suits, white collared shirts and ties.

"Hiya, fellas," I said with a forced smile. "I'm here for dinner."

The two men continued to approach. One was on the left side of me. The other was on the right side of me. They were muscular, hardened men, I could tell. They were probably ex-military, I guessed.

The one on the left side of me slowed.

"What's your name?"

"Cam," I said. "Cameron Weaver."

"Yeah, got you," the man said, looking at a notebook computer he was carrying and then to his partner. The second man slowed and switched from his initial aggression to something less aggressive. "Would you follow me?" The second man asked.

"Sure," I said, looking at the man beside me who looked like he was ready to jump on a hand grenade if necessary. "What's with all the security?"

"Just precautions," the man beside me with the tablet said. "Important people get a lot of unwanted attention. We are here to make sure everyone has a good time without any distractions."

"Okay," I said, confused. "Everyone?"

The pair of security men dropped me at the front door to another man dressed in a dark suit and earpiece. I introduced myself and after a light frisking entered the palatial home of the Hudson's.

To call it palatial did no justice to the expansive and eye-popping home. The two-story home was breath taking. Standing in the foyer I was stunned at the opulence. The foyer was all marble and columns and had one of those staircases that split halfway up to allow you to go left or right to the second floor. It was like I was on a TV set instead of the inside of someone's home.

The second story of the house led God knows where. I noted at least half a dozen doors on the second floor and art pieces scattered above my head. Above my head, in the foyer, was a chandelier that looked like it should have been in a museum instead of Henderson, Nevada.

Music was playing from somewhere and that only added to the TV feeling of the experience. The art on the walls was very familiar and I wanted to believe that I had seen some of it in museums, but that was not possible. The ceilings seemed to be built for someone seven or eight feet tall. I could not help but stare and try to take in the splendor of the home.

I focused on the first floor and found one of those acrylic balloon animals that had been made by some artist and cost a boatload of money just off the foyer. There were several paintings I knew I had seen in books, hanging on the walls of the Hudson home. I tried to calculate just how much all the art was worth when a sand-colored woman, dressed all in black, walked up to me.

She was thin and athletic redbone woman who moved like a gymnast with a short curly faux Mohawk with shaved sides. In her ears were medium sized gold stud earrings. She looked a little like Zoe Saldana and Nathalie Emmanuel or a mix of the two I thought. I probably thought that because of her hazel eyes.

"Young Cameron Weaver? My name is Larissa," the woman said with an English accent and a slight grin.

"Cameron?" I recoiled at the word. "Naw, please don't call me that. I'm Cam. Please?"

"Right, sorry. Cam," the woman smiled, her hazel eyes playful beneath perfectly arched eyebrows. "If you will follow me, the family is waiting for you on the patio."

I followed the stranger into the bowels of the continually unfolding home. We walked past the area that had a gigantic half circle leather sofa which sat in front of a wall which offered the mouth of a fireplace. Above the fireplace was a painting of some artist. On the right side of the leather couch was another area that was reached by a short staircase to what looked like a conference room. The conference room was glassed in and there was a black table in the room that was filled with books and trophies and some high-backed chairs.

As we proceeded, I could see at least a dozen men and women busying themselves in the interior. I looked to the left and saw the dining room or what looked like the dining room. Again, I assumed it was the dining room because there was a long table with a floral arrangement that sat in the center of the table and above the table hung another jaw dropping chandelier.

In less than five minutes I was in the rear of the Hudson home. What dominated the rear of the house was the Olympic size swimming pool. I followed and looked at the exercise room at one corner of the house. On the other corner was the restaurant pretending to be a kitchen. In between the exercise room was what looked like a small artist studio. On the far side of the house, just off the kitchen was another room that looked like a café.

Outside, there was a firepit set ablaze and the family sitting around it. They were laughing and talking when I arrived. Kyla was sitting next to a woman that looked like an older version of her, except she had shoulder length straightened hair and a slightly lighter complexion. Next to the older version of Kyla was a handsome young man, maybe in his late twenties, dressed in a blazer and turtleneck. He was wearing blue jeans and lace up shoes. Next to him was a stunningly beautiful black woman with a V-shaped face framed by short puffy curls. She was striking because when she turned the woman was wearing bright red lipstick on her full lips. She was wearing a denim top, jeans and boots. Hanging from her ears were thin hoop earrings. The last man, I assumed it was Mister Hudson, Kyla's father, had his back to me as I stepped onto the patio. He was a stocky man dressed in sweater and jeans.

Kyla, upon seeing me, climbed to her feet and ran to my side. She was wearing cable knit sweater, jeans and sneakers. I smiled seeing Kyla. I was glad she remembered me.

The woman who had escorted me to the patio smiled and seeing Kyla's reaction turned and walked away without a word. I noted that the nameless woman in black was wearing an earpiece. I assumed she was security.

"I can't believe you are here," Kyla said with a big hug and squeeze that surprised me. She instantly released me and turned and holding my hand marched us toward the six people sitting near the firepit.

I had all these one liners in my head but chose not to say anything. I need to feel out the crowd. I looked at Kyla and smiled.

"Looks like a tough crowd," I said.

"They can be," Kyla said.

"I think I can handle them," I said as we walked toward the firepit to meet the family.

The issue, if there was an issue, was her mom and dad. The Hudson's were this upper crust family in Henderson that everyone knew and wanted to be like.

Kyla did the introductions. I listened and smiled and shook hands with Mister Hudson and his son. I nodded to Kyla's mother and the woman next to her.

"Thank you for coming up," Kyle Hudson, Mister Hudson, Kyla's father, said, watching me like I might steal something. He was a round faced man in his late forties, I guessed. He had an intense stare that reminded me of Medusa for some reason. You could not look at him directly too long, I mused. He was clean shaven and had a tapered fade etched on his round head. Mister Hudson wasn't very tall, but stocky and thickly built.

"No, thank you sir, for inviting me to meet you," I said, with a smile.

"You work, Cam?"

"No, sir," I said. "I'm still in high school. I am trying to prepare for college," I added.

He was all about money. He seemed to be weighing my value as he talked. He was very direct and believed his money insulated him from reprisal.

"Where do you live Cam?"

"In Henderson, sir," I said.

"You planning on going to UNLV?"

"I'm not sure sir, still trying to figure it out," I said.

Mister Hudson poked out his lip with that reply. He fell silent.

"Not everyone has their life all planned out Kyle," his wife said.

"It's good to have a plan," Mister Hudson said. "You never know what is around the next corner."

"You didn't plan on running into me at UNLV," his wife said. "We didn't plan on starting a family right out of college," she added. "We don't really plan our family life too much, Cam."

"That's not true," Mister Hudson said.

"We didn't plan on having junior right away," Missus Hudson said with a smile. "That worked out despite not planning."

I listened and wanted to laugh. Kyla's mother was surprisingly witty.

"Don't mind them, Cam," Kyle Junior said. "They love to pull each other's chains, for some reason."

I smiled at the supposed heir to the Hudson empire. Kyle Junior, twenty something, who was recently married to the one-time personality and Instagram model Jennifer Benton. They had both went to UNLV and fallen in love while there. Or so the story went.

"Jen and I got married before we graduated," Kyle Junior said. "My dad was not too happy about the decision."

"Why?"

"He had other plans," the son of Mister Hudson said.

I nodded.

"They threatened to disown Kay Jay, initially," Jennifer said, in a whisper.

"It was just a threat," Kyle Junior said with a thin smile. "Obviously," the son said, with a smile. "It is how he determines if we care."

The conversation quickly turned to real estate.

"You know son that you and Jennifer should be considering moving out of Vegas and out to Henderson. You get more land for your money," Mister Hudson said.

"I know. I know," Junior Hudson said. "It's just that we like where we are right now. It suits our needs."

"Well, things change," Mister Hudson said.

"That's true," Kyle Junior said with a knowing smile. "We have to be ready for change or get plowed under trying to fight it."

"That's true. Don't change just to change though," Mister Hudson said. "Change to suit you and the needs of others." Mister Hudson paused. "Stubbornness and ignorance can be worse than doing nothing."

I listened not sure what the two Hudson men were talking about suddenly. They both seemed intense and determined. I wondered, to what extent the family would go to stop my attention to their only daughter?

We moved to the dining room and under the watchful eyes of half a dozen security members we ate. Of course, I wanted to ask about the security, but I didn't.

Kyla's father ate and toyed with me while he ate.

"Do you like school?"

I smiled at the question. I got good grades in school. Mister Hudson reminded me of a bunch of my teachers. He was asking questions he already knew the answer to, just to test me.

"I do," I said, to Mister Hudson, smiling and not shoveling in my food as I usually did.

"Do you like the food?"

"Yes, sir, I do," I said. "Thank you very much. My compliments to the chef."

"I will have the chef come to the table before he and his staff leave," Mister Hudson said, looking at me through his dark eyes.

He looked away and with a gesture one of his men scurried to his side. He whispered something and the man retreated into the recesses of the mansion.

There were four plates served after the appetizers and salads and then the after salad before dinner.

"You like our home, Cam?"

"Yes, sir, I do," I said. I watched as a man dressed in a chef's hat, white apron and carrying hand towel. Behind him followed four others with dishes.

As the fourth plate was served the chef and his crew were packing out and the security was focused on the departure of the half dozen strangers exiting the residence.

I was treated to the Frago Agri Doce chicken meal.

I watched Kyla's father and brother as I ate. If they used their forks, I used my fork. I figured they couldn't be mad at me for imitating their eating habits. So, I ate and enjoyed the chicken meal and the small talk.

I paused as the chef arrived at the table and told us the meal we were about to enjoy. He was some well-known chef from the Rodizio Brazilian Steakhouse.

"Good evening and thank you for the opportunity to serve you and your family tonight, Mister Hudson," the chef said, with a bow.

"Thank you, chef," Mister Hudson said.

Everyone was served their last course, a dessert. The dessert was a choice of two chocolate extravagances. Torta Brigadeiro and Bolo Brigadeiro. Torta Brigadeiro was a slice of decadent chocolate mousse torte, made with a blend of four chocolate. The Torta Brigadeiro was gluten-free for those who worried about that. This treat was served ala mode with sliced bananas and fresh whipped cream. The second choice was the Bolo Brigadeiro. This dessert was a three-layer chocolate cake with an avalanche of warm Brigadeiro sauce, bananas, ice cream and whipped cream.

Of course, I chose the Bolo Brigadeiro and so did Kyla. We made googly eyes at each other while we ate our dessert. Her father, the ever-serious Kyle Hudson, pretended not to notice. Her mother, Angela Hudson, smiled as she ate her Torta Brigadeiro.

The woman, Larissa, all in black, appeared again and said that the team was moving to perimeter surveillance, whatever that was.

The breadwinner of the Hudson family nodded. The woman departed. We ate and I watched Kyla out of the corner of my eye seeing if she was doing all right. She ate delicately like her mother and Junior's wife.

After Larissa talked to Mister Hudson the table seemed to relax.

In my head, I ticked off a few things I wanted to ask Kyla when we were alone. How many people are guarding the family every day? How many guards watch Kyla daily? When Kyla is at school, are security there? Is the house always guarded? Does the family travel with guards? Are they all armed? Have they ever had to defend themselves at their home? Do they have a panic room? The questions that filled my head seemed endless.

I blinked, trying to refocus on the dinner and Kyla and her family.

In my distraction Mister Hudson had been speaking, but mostly small talk. I looked and found Mister Hudson looking at me intently. I knew I had missed something.

"What do you say Cameron?"

"Excuse me, sir?"

"Do you have an opinion?"

"Could you repeat your question, sir?"

"Surely," Mister Hudson said. "I was saying that the passing down of inheritance is essential, especially for those building wealth. My question was simply isn't there being a need for merit-based inheritance instead of biological inheritance. I was curious of your opinion?"

"Well, sir, I most assuredly have no understanding of inheritance or the need for merit-based or biological inheritance," I said, thinking that was the end of that.

Then Mister Hudson showed me his nature. The realtor smiled and nodded and then looked to his son before speaking.

"Well, Cameron, biological inheritance, in my opinion, was the throwback idea that goes back to the royal families and monarchies," Mister Hudson said.

I listened. Everyone at the table listened. Kyle Junior seemed to squirm a bit.

"The problem with the biological strategy is that unearned riches breeds contempt and laziness. Too often those heirs are not driven to challenge themselves. They are content, in general, with the riches destined to come to them." Mister Hudson paused. "Are you familiar with trust fund babies?"

I nodded. I had heard the term used before by someone.

"Well, the richest have secured a leisure class of ultra-rich do nothings. Imagine if you will people with no talent but incredible caches of money and influence, attempting to run businesses with only their name and money as their backing," Mister Hudson said, shaking his head at the thought. "I suggest that merit-based inheritance is a better plan."

"Why?"

"It is a better use of the money and wealth," Mister Hudson said. "It is given to the heir or employee or whoever that is the most industrious," Mister Hudson said, with an insidious smile.

"How do you determine who is the most industrious, sir?"

"Good question," Mister Hudson said with a wry smile. "I suppose it is all subjective, but to protect the wealth that has been amassed I would think there would be lawyers and accountants involved."

"Would the heirs still get a trust fund?" Kyla asked with a smile.

"I suppose," Mister Hudson said.

"That's very interesting, sir," I said, eating as everyone at the table continued eating and watching Mister Hudson.

After dinner, we all sat at the dining table and talked. Kyle Junior seemed to be fuming for some reason. His wife was talking to him quietly. Mister Hudson climbed to his feet and everyone at the table followed suit. He walked to the living room, where the gigantic couch rested, and stood in front of the mantle and the incredibly large picture of his family framed above it.

The Hudson's sat and lounged on the couch. I sat next to Kyla.

"You, okay?" I asked Kyla. She seemed a little nervous, like she was about to take a math test. I reached out and held her hand. Touching her hand, Kyla smiled and seemed to recall I was there.

"I'm okay," Kyla said. "How are you doing?"

"I guess I'm okay," I said.

"Cameron, I hope you have enjoyed yourself," Mister Hudson said.

I smiled. I could tell this was the moment. He had fed me. Now, Mister Hudson was going to try and dissect me.

"What do you want from our Kyla?" Mister Hudson asked.

I smiled at the question as everyone on the couch tensed. I knew it was coming. It had to come, I figured. He was her dad. He was trying to protect his money. He was trying to protect his daughter too, maybe. The way he was looking at me, like I was a bug in his house that needed to be stepped on, only made me think how I wanted to answer the question.

In my head I knew I had just three ways to answer Kyle Hudson. He was this powerful guy that thought his money made him important. To him, his money was the reason he woke. I knew people like him. I couldn't lie and say I knew people as rich and powerful as him. I didn't. I just knew the type.

He was all about his money and figured, by extension, everyone in his circle was around him for his money. So, I could *have said that the money he had meant nothing to me, which was true, but for someone like Kyle Hudson he wouldn't believe that. He would think I was lying.*

The second choice I had as an answer for the most powerful black realtor in Las Vegas was to tell him I didn't know. Of course, not knowing, in Kyla's father's mind, was weakness. Again, knowing the type I knew that he mapped out everything. I was guaranteed he was already thinking about the boy that he would accept dating Kyla.

Mister Hudson probably, in some subtle way, had planned out Kyla's life, to a certain extent. I was sure that Hudson told his son Jennifer Benson was the one. He liked to wield power even when it had nothing to do with him. I looked at the man looking at me and knew that in his mind there was never a time that things were not about him.

So, I chose the third option. I looked at Kyle Hudson and smiled.

"Well, sir," I said, looking Mister Hudson in the eye. "I don't know how to answer that," I said with a smile. "I guess I want to say that I just want to hang out with your daughter and see what happens." I paused. Angela Hudson smile melted just a little. Kyle Junior frowned. Kyla looked amused.

"I can't say that I have some simple, pat answer, really, sir. This is all still pretty new for me," I said. I rubbed my hands on my jeans, nervously. "I think that I would love to just spend as much time as I can with your daughter, to get to know her better." I paused, thinking. "I've never had a girlfriend before, sir. So, I want to just hang with her, if that makes any sense. I just want to get to know her." I smiled at Kyla who was smiling at me.

I looked at Mister Hudson who was staring at me like I had just broken something in their house.

"I like your daughter, sir. She's funny." I shrugged. "She's nerdy, like me," I added. "She makes me laugh." I smiled at Kyla, and she smiled back.

"Sometimes," I looked at Kyla who was still smiling. "Sometimes, I make her laugh. For me, that's good enough. I mean, I'm seventeen." I shook my head, confused. "We've been together for less than a week. Right?" I looked to Kyla. She nodded even though she seemed petrified at what I was saying.

"I just want to hang with her, nothing more." I looked at Kyla's father who was smiling like a lion might in front of a T-bone steak. I looked to Kyla, then her mother and brother and his wife.

"I mean, you should ask Kyla what she wants from me," I said. "I'm pretty simple."

That was that.

Missus Hudson was nice. She smiled and giggled when I finished. Kyle Junior was a bit of a stuffed shirt and shook his head and reached out to hold his wife's hand. His wife was pretty to look at, but nothing beyond that. I was not sure if she had even listened to what I had said.

Kyle Hudson studied me and there was an uncomfortable silence as he weighed my response in his head. He looked to Kyla and then to his wife and finally his son. When he returned his gaze to me, I noticed a subtle difference in his look. He didn't say anything about what I had said. He just nodded.

The only person that mattered, to me, was Kyla Hudson. She was smiling one of those smiles that you see when you have been gone for a long time and then you see someone again. I smiled too. Kyla climbed to her feet and dragged me out of the living room and away from the eyes of her family.

"Let me take you on a tour," Kyla said. I shrugged and followed.

Kyla took me on a tour of the mansion. It was just incredible. With most of the security gone the mansion seemed even more expansive. We walked through the main floor, and I just marveled at the space.

On the second floor of the mansion were four of the five bedrooms. Her parents' bedroom was on the second floor and *looked like an apartment all to itself. The other three bedrooms were not small. Each bedroom had windows directed toward the desert and the mountains beyond. The view, that night was tranquil as the dark horizon and mountains sat there some miles away from the home.*

Yet, it was Kyla's bedroom that surprised me the most. I didn't know what I was expecting, but the eggshell white walls and the framed art was not on my list. There was no canopied bed. No girly accessories. Instead, she had a desk next to the wall that led to the sliding door and private balcony.

"It's nice," I said.

Kyla smiled and I was mesmerized by the twist of her lips and gloss. She stepped forward and tried to hug me. Seeing her approach, I awkwardly reached out for Kyla. We innocently met in the space vacated by our lips.

I held Kyla Hudson and tasted her bubblegum and honey sweet lips. She wrapped her arms around my neck.

"What was that for?"

"I don't know," she said with a big smile. "No one stands up to my daddy."

"I can't believe that," I said.

"I'm serious," Kyla said.

"That's crazy," I said. "How does he know his..." I trailed off not sure what to say suddenly.

Bored with the conversation she leaned forward and kissed me again, this time deeply and seriously.

I had wanted to kiss Kyla the moment I had seen her but refrained. I figured her father might see that as a party foul. I was holding her by her waist and feeling a little uncomfortable below the waist as things started to percolate. I closed my eyes trying to stop my body from betraying my thoughts. That did not work. I pulled back and shook my head like there was something in my ear.

"Ky, we can't do this here," I said, pulling back from my incredibly sexy girlfriend.

"We're just kissing," she said, her arms locked around my neck.

I reached up and pulled her arms away. I looked at her, annoyed. She smiled impishly in response. Kyla was this incredibly bright and beautiful person but with a bit of a wild side. I didn't see that wild side immediately, but there were signs.

When I finally left the Hudson estate Kyla gave me a hug and small kiss on my cheek and smiled wickedly again.

"Hope that was okay," Kyla said, looking down below my waistline.

I shook my head and rubbed the back of my neck.

"Yeah, sure," I said with a laugh. "Thanks for everything," I said and climbed into the Jetta.

When I got home my mom was waiting. She didn't prod or poke as I expected.

She let me go to my bedroom and come back to the kitchen before saying:

"Well, if you like her and she likes you," she said, turning and putting away a dish she had just washed. "I suppose I should meet her."

"Aw, mom," I said.

"What?"

"Nothing," I said.

"You ashamed of me?"

"Not even," I said with a laugh and hugged her.

"You better not," my mother said.

I laughed. How could I be ashamed of my mother? I released her and walked to the living room and sat down on the couch. I sat and reached for the TV remote and paused. I looked around the modest interior of our home. I liked our home. I liked every bit of it. It felt like me and my mom.

        I liked the idea of being Kyla Hudson's boyfriend. It took a little getting used to, but I was nothing if not malleable. Two weeks turned into one month. In high school, one month is like one hundred months anywhere else. There were all these traps and pitfalls laid by others to trip me and Kyla up. Thankfully, we didn't give in. We weren't perfect. There were moments.

Chapter 2.

Nearly three weeks after the Hudson dinner that seemed more like an inquisition than dinner and a couple of weeks after a private meeting with her dad Kyla decided to be rambunctious. She was always complaining about being a prisoner. I thought it was a bad idea. I said as much. But when Kyla got an idea in her head it was almost impossible to dissuade her. She was a steaming locomotive barreling down the tracks and whoever got in her way was inevitable roadkill.

So, that day at lunch, I walked to the table to see Wes, Justice and Lyle. They were unimpressed with the whole Kyla relationship thing by then.

"What up?"

"Your girl needs you?"

I turned and saw Kyla dressed in a Warriors basketball jersey waving me over to her table.

"She has something to ask me?" I asked Wes. In response, he rolled his eyes.

Lyle, eating his lunch, shook his head, disapprovingly.

"You can't let her run you like that," Lyle said, never having a girlfriend longer than a week.

"Girls want someone telling them what is what," he added.

Justice sat and watched Wes and Lyle. When I looked at him, he smiled and nodded.

"Do her parents like you?"

"Yeah, I'm adorable," I said with a snicker.

"I don't see it," Wes said. "I think she's getting back at her dad or something with you."

"I think she's punishing her dad," Lyle said, with a handful of chips in his hands. "I guarantee he's turning flips at night thinking of things that are wrong with you."

"I have to go. I mean, I love to hear all the reasons why you aren't happy for me and Ky, but I have to go and talk with my girlfriend instead of making up a bunch of wacky conspiracy theories with my delusional friends I've known since I was maybe seven," I said and shook my head. I turned on my heels and walked away from the lunch table and across the cafeteria to Kyla.

When Kyla saw me approaching, she climbed up from the table and headed for the exit. I followed. In the hallway she seemed upset.

"What's wrong?"

"I think my dad doesn't like you," Kyla said in the hallway.

I let that sink in. I didn't respond instantly. Instead, I looked at my girlfriend of seven days and smiled.

"So?"

"So, if he doesn't like you then he will figure out a way to make you stop seeing me."

"That's not happening," I said, looking at Kyla. "Wait. You still like me? Right?"

"Of course," Kyla said.

"Well, then nothing else matters."

"What do you mean?"

"I mean, the only people that matter are right here in this hallway. When you stop liking me then I'll start worrying. If I stop liking you then you can start worrying. That fair?"

Kyla smiled and nodded.

"How you so smart?"

"It's my mom, I think," I said, with a crooked smile. I was close enough to Kyla that I could count her freckles on her cheek. Being that close I could also see that she had a dimple just beneath her right jawbone.

She hugged me. I hugged her back.

I thought, here I am with the prettiest girl at Foothill High School, and she wants me to get in trouble with her. We were going to ditch her two bodyguards at Foothill and head for... God knows where. In my teenage brain it seemed harmless enough. What was the worst thing that could happen?

Stupid. Stupid. Stupid.

She was the daughter of Kyle Hudson, the owner of Hudson Realtors, one of the biggest black real estate agencies in Henderson. Her father, the three or four times I met him, was powerful, all business, self-absorbed real estate magnate who seemed to be always thinking of a way to land the next big deal. Always dressed impeccably. Always wreaking of power and control. He was nice, if you considered being grilled by someone who could have you killed and buried in the desert, and no one would know about it, nice. He was not overtly intimidating but there was this tension and hypersensitivity when he was around that said tons.

From what I got from Kyla her father was always business driven. He loved his family. He loved all the things that his job afforded for him and his family. Yet, he was obsessed with staying on top of the real estate heap he had amassed.

Her mother, Missus Angela Hudson, was a beautiful woman who, and according to Kyla, had met Mister Hudson in college and gotten married before they graduated. The pair had traveled east for a few years attempting to carve out a name for themselves in New York and then Boston. Yet, it had been on a Las Vegas trip that Mister Hudson saw the light. He was a salesman and looked at the untapped potential of Las Vegas and decided then and there to become a realtor.

Missus Hudson loved telling of the rags to riches story of her and her ultra-successful husband.

"In just five years my Kyle had gained a grip on the often-overlooked black real estate market in Clark County," Missus Hudson said. *"He had scrambled and gained a foothold on a market that was being underserved."*

She loved to make these dramatic pauses, when she talked about anything.

"In Las Vegas, if you weren't buying and selling million-dollar homes and billion-dollar properties you were not given the time of day. Hudson concentrated on the properties that others brushed off and gained a loyal clientele. The sixth year in Las Vegas my Kyle bought his first million-dollar home. A year later, he sold it and bought the home in Henderson where we live now."

"He was unquestionably the hardest working realtor in Las Vegas," Missus Hudson said, with a slight grin. "He is always working on some project. I think he is presently working on a big project with some east coast investors trying to buy a casino and hotel that would cement his rise in the real estate industry. Kyle is unquestionably the biggest black real estate agent in Las Vegas."

Angela Hudson had worked with her husband and built-up Hudson Realtors from a storefront in North Las Vegas to the three-story building in Henderson. They employed nearly thirty realtors and over sixty employees. Angela Hudson was the office manager. Well, she had been until the birth of her first child, Kyle Junior. Angela Hudson took time off and Kyle Hudson redoubled his efforts to become the most successful black realtor in Las Vegas. He hired Veronica English, temporarily, to fill in for Angela while she was on maternity leave.

Junior Hudson was five, going on six, when Angela told Kyle she was pregnant with Kyla. Kyle Hudson was elated. Again, Kyle called upon Veronica English to fill in for Angela. This time she would take on an assistant role and eventually, became the office manager, a few years later.

Missus Hudson found herself focusing on family. Junior Hudson, the heir apparent, went to UNLV and got a degree in business administration. He got his degree with the hope and belief that one day he would take over his father's business, eventually. While at UNLV, Junior was in a car accident and nearly *killed. The car accident and all the police reports and court records had magically disappeared.*

Kyla, the second child and daughter, was this fairytale princess locked away in a castle and protected by... her dad and her dad's money. At sixteen, she decided to ditch her bodyguards for the day and go to the Galleria with me in my Volkswagen Jetta. I had almost forgotten that Kyla Hudson was the daughter of Kyle Hudson, one of the most powerful men in Henderson, Nevada.

Her father was one of a handful of black realtors that carved out a footprint in the sands outside of Las Vegas and thrived while others were trying to break into the nearly impossible Las Vegas real estate.

Hudson had quietly developed deals in Henderson for nearly twenty years and now found himself one of the movers and shakers of Henderson.

Kyla merited a bodyguard and a driver because of her father's success. The real estate game was cutthroat. The thirty smaller realtors were always looking for an advantage. Initially, they had used cold calls and block parties to find new clients. Then it had been bus bench ads and billboards. Now, it was TV ads.

Everyone in Las Vegas and Henderson had seen at least one of the Hudson ads.

The latest ads had Kyle Hudson and his wife and kids were in them. The TV ad began simply with a man or woman sitting at a café or in their cramped apartment looking for a home on their computer. In the café Kyle Hudson would sit beside the man or woman dressed like a million bucks with that used car salesman smile of his. In the cramped apartment the doorbell would ring, and Kyle Hudson would be standing there dressed like a storefront preacher in a thousand-dollar suit. He would explain the best way to buy a house was through the tried-and-true Hudson way.

The commercial would end with the tagline, "We'll get you into your dream house. You just have to see it to believe it. We're always working for you."

At math class Kyla leaned over and put her hand on mine. We held hands occasionally, but we weren't heavy into PDA. So, when she touched my hand, I was a little taken aback. I looked and saw her looking serious.

She had her devious look on her face.

"I think we need to get away from here, for a little bit," Kyla said, in a whisper. "Afterschool."

"What about Eddy and the others?"

"What about them?"

"They aren't going to let you just leave," I said.

"They don't show up until school lets out," Kyla said. She was already planning out our escape.

"Ky, you know that school is locked down?"

"Cam, if we can get out will you go with me?"

I smiled. Of the two of us I was the only one with a car. I closed my eyes and wished that Kyla was suddenly a dream.

"Cam let's get out of here," Kyla said as class let out. We were in the chaos of a period change. Hundreds of students were moving back in forth in the halls.

I looked at my beautiful girlfriend and tried to think of something to say that made sense.

"I just need a break from all the security and people watching me."

I understood. Well, I understood how crazy it had to be for Kyla living in casa de Hudson and all the security around her all the time. It was one of our conversations that never ended. Kyla would want to go out and one or two people had to go with her wherever she went.

Though we didn't live in Los Angeles or Las Vegas it felt like people were always trying to get close to Kyla. There weren't paparazzi, but there were the curious and obnoxious who wanted to know who was in the SUV or merited bodyguards.

Her father had given her some flexibility, in terms of bodyguards. She had her own bodyguards. Eddy Danielson, the short and powerfully built ex-Marine was the guy that usually picked her up from Foothill. The driver was another no neck ex-military guy named Lloyd Colson. In all the time I had been going out with Kyla, Colson had said a handful of words to me. The last was the Larissa Wolfe. She had been reassigned after the meeting with Mister Hudson. She told me, personally, that she was there "to protect Kyla's virtue."

"What does that mean?"

"Got me," Larissa said with a shrug of her shoulders. "I'm just paid to do what her dad tells me."

Of the three, Larissa Wolfe seemed to have a personality. The other two were just bricks ready to hurt anyone that got too close to Kyla.

"You know Larissa is going to be pissed if you try and ghost her," I said.

Kyla shrugged her shoulders.

"You sure about this?"

"I just need a break," Kyla said.

I reluctantly agreed.

Kyla grabbed my hand and we walked to the gymnasium, like we were going to gym class. As soon as we got near the gym, we slipped out of one of the side doors that led to the school parking lot. Kyla dressed in a gray T-shirt, blue jeans and basketball sneakers did a pirouette once out of doors. I smiled.

We walked toward my parked car. In the parking lot there were already buses lining up to take students to various parts of Henderson. I looked left and right and was surprised to see parents already lined up to pick up their children.

That commercial was in my head when Kyla climbed into my car and told me to drive. I loved how spontaneous Kyla could be. It was one of the things that attracted me to her besides her dimples, pouty lips and drop-dead gorgeous looks. It didn't hurt that she was wicked smart and one of the richest kids at Foothill. But the money thing never was a factor for me. I didn't care about money. I know how it sounds having said all that about Kyla and her money, but I was serious. I understood the significance of money, but I was not driven by it. I was not materialistic. At least, I did not believe I was.

"Perfect timing," Kyla said.

"I don't know about all that," I said, unlocking the Jetta and letting Kyla inside.

I climbed in my car and started the engine.

Instantly, my stereo started blaring some rap music lyrics. I reached out and lowered the volume.

"Sorry," I said, with a slight frown that quickly turned to a smile.

"Vamenos muchacho," Kyla said with a broad smile.

I put the Jetta into gear and drove to the parking lot exit. The security guard assigned to the parking lot was talking to one of the bus drivers as we exited the parking lot.

As I headed to the parking lot exit there was no Eddy to raise a hand to stop me.

I had not had to slow at the gate to Foothill High School, because the security guards had unlocked the gates to allow the buses time to line up to take students across Henderson. In the influx of buses, I drove my Jetta out of the campus undetected.

Kyla giggled in the passenger seat as the Jetta drove away from the high school.

So, Thursday, the week after homecoming, I drove Kyla out of the parking lot of Foothill before Eddy, her bodyguard, arrived to pick her up.

"You are going to get Eddy in all sorts of trouble," I said as we drove out of the parking lot and onto the main street.

"No. It's cool. My dad hired him," Kyla said in the passenger seat beside me. "They know that there are times that I need a little space. That's why I have a cellphone. If there's an emergency, then I can call them." She paused and looked at the street we were driving on. "Can we go to the mall?"

"The mall? Seriously?"

"Yeah, what's wrong with going to the mall?"

I refused to answer.

The Galleria at Sunset was one of the biggest indoor malls in Henderson, Nevada. We, Kyla and I, drove past two other malls to get to the Galleria at Sunset. I figured what the eff? If she got in trouble then she would have someone to be in trouble with, namely me.

We got there and the first place Kyla wanted to go was to Build-A-Bear. I can't remember how many times I had been in the mall and walked past Build-A-Bear and seen all those little whiny kids and said, in my head, not on my life. But Kyla dragged me inside and we both made a bear.

"Is that why you wanted to come here?"

"Sort of," Kyla said with a teasing smile.

"Why?"

My bear was for my mom. It was yellow and with a tiara. I thought my mother's bear looked pretty good for the first bear I had ever made.

Of course, there was no contest between Kyla's bear and my bear. She had made a pink bear with eyelashes, hoop earrings, pearl necklace, dress and little handbag. The extra details made the bear distinct.

In fact, as I was finishing my yellow bear for my mom Kyla had begun and was finishing her second creation. The second bear was a dark brown bear wearing a watch and carrying a briefcase. The second bear was for her dad.

After making the bears and paying we walked around the mall and stopped at a few stores.

"Why did you want to come here?"

Kyla shook her head, instead of answering. I didn't push. We walked into a department store and browsed the aisles. Kyla went to the young women's department. I slowed and decided to go to the men's department.

"Don't get lost," Kyla said with a chuckle.

I didn't answer. I walked around the department store and after a few minutes met Kyla by the perfume counter. She was being helped by one of the fragrance representatives.

"Would you like to try this one sir?"

I lifted my hands to the woman with the atomizer and tried to navigate the perfume counter.

"I'm going to be over there," I said to Kyla and made a beeline for the shoe department that was just on the edge of the perfume counter for some reason.

"Can I help you, sir?"

I turned and found myself face-to-face with a square faced, Elvis Presley-like pompadour wearing, high forehead college age man wearing wire-rimmed glasses, light blue collared shirt, nametag, brown leather belt, dark blue pants and matching brown leather lace-up shoes.

"I'm just waiting for my--," I said, looking at the shoe salesman.

Before the salesman could start Kyla appeared and saved me.

"Have a good day," I said to the salesman as we left the department store.

Kyla smiled and laughed.

"Thanks for the save," I said. "I hate going into those stores. They are all sell, sell, sell."

"I don't know, it's not that big a deal. I like the attention," Kyla said.

I slowed at her words.

"What?"

Kyla hesitated.

"You like the attention but then how did we get here?"

"I don't always like all the attention," Kyla said, correcting herself.

"Yeah, maybe it's not the attention you don't like," I said, thinking. "It's the control."

"Yeah, maybe."

"Yeah, definitely."

"I don't know how you do it," I said to Kyla as we walked toward the food court.

School had let out and five minutes after school was out, she received her first set of phone calls. Kyla ignored all the phone calls and then the text messages started coming in.

"You aren't going to answer the phone?"

"No. They all know that every so often I need a break."

"They know?"

"Well, they should," Kyla said.

"Well, if your dad had it in for me before, now he's going to have a real reason," I said.

"No, he's not going to blame you. There's enough blame to go around already," Kyla said.

We grabbed some Chinese on the second level in the food court and while we were eating Kyla decided to turn off her phone.

"You know that a lot of people try to control me? From my dad on down to the men that work for him."

I nodded.

"They are so annoying," she said.

"So, what do you want to do?"

"Well, I could torture them more, but I know you aren't enjoying this as much as I am," Kyla said. "I suppose we could head back." She paused. "You can take me back to my house."

"You sure?"

Kyla smiled at my question. It looked like she was about to burst out laughing. Instead, she reached out and placed a hand on my cheek.

"I know you and I want my family to like you, Cam. I really want that too. But they want to decide on who I like and don't like. They want to control me. That control thing of my dad is too much, at times. He decides all the things in the house."

"That's crazy. You are *his* daughter. You aren't *his* robot," I said. "I mean, you aren't a *robot*? Right?"

Kyla laughed.

"Sometimes the only way that I can be free is doing the unexpected," Kyla said with a laugh.

"That's not good," I said, thinking about what she had said.

"It's not good," Kyla said, agreeing. She reached out and held my hand.

I listened. I was glad Kyla wanted to go home. There were a bunch of people searching for her. I figured that the quickest way for her to get control was to confront her dad head-on, but that was a conversation for another day.

It was maybe five o'clock when we decided to leave the mall. We had only been there for less than two hours, but it seemed like forever and no time at all.

I had the bears and a couple of bags of things Kyla had bought and we were headed back to my car when a guy stepped in front of Kyla and smiled. He had a gun in his hand.

I thought it was a robbery. I stepped forward to protect Kyla but someone from behind hit me and I bounced off a car and dropped all the packages.

"Don't do anything stupid, bee--," the guy said with the gun.

Out of the corner of my eye another guy wearing an oversized watch and a chain with a pistol medallion around his neck, grabbed my collar and punched me.

"Night, night, Romeo," the crooked nosed brawler said through gold teeth.

Then everything went black.

Chapter 3.

When I opened my eyes the first person I saw was the dark eyed Larissa Wolfe. She was standing beside me, looking angry. She had her hands in her jacket and was listening to someone talking I couldn't see. Larissa looked down seeing me looking at her and placed a hand on my shoulder. The movement caught the attention of someone and suddenly Eddy was standing over me, holding the remains of Kyla's phone in his hand.

Larissa Wolfe stayed beside me and continued to look disturbed.

I sat up and realized I was in a small office with about four other people. I scanned the room and realized that I was in a mall security office. The four people dressed in dark uniforms like police all had a walkie talkie, earpiece and a stern look on their face.

There were two older men with crewcuts and square jaws who looked like they were just out of the Marines. One of them had a mustache and looked a little like Jim Carey. The other crew cut had sideburns and wore dark horn-rimmed glasses. They were broad shouldered men who seemed to be borderline gym rats. They had big biceps and wore short sleeve shirts.

The other two men were smaller versions of the square jawed gym rats. One of the younger gym rats had long blonde hair that fell to his shoulders. The other had his hair in a kind of a short brown moppish haircut.

"You okay?"

I looked at Eddy and Larissa and then to the older gym rat with the mustache who was speaking.

"Easy, tiger," Larissa Wolfe said.

"How long has he been here?"

"Well, we got a call that someone was unconscious in the mall," the mustached crew cut guy said.

"It can't have been more than ten or fifteen minutes," the moppish security guard said with his thumbs hooked in his utility belt.

"The way we heard it this young man was mugged leaving the mall. He's lucky he's alive," the man with the sideburns said with a smirk.

I looked around the sparsely furnished room and saw a desk, four chairs, a bank of radios and above the radios six monitors. There were a small group of storage lockers. On the other side of the lockers, I found the three Build-A-Bears sitting in a chair near another set of lockers.

I rubbed the side of my face, and the right side was tender to the touch. I touched my right eye and winced.

"Yeah, you might want to be a little easy checking yourself out," the second security guard said.

Eddy looked around and then checked his phone.

"We'll be leaving," Eddy said.

Larissa walked over to the Build-A-Bears and grabbed them.

"Can you sign this report?"

Eddy smirked and pushed past the two security officers to the door. He pushed open the door and did not look back. Eddy pushed past the next three security guards. The square jawed crewcut leader stepped aside as Eddy moved out of the small office.

Larissa pushed me forward and wordlessly we exited.

"How do we get in contact with you?"

I looked back, but Larissa placed a hand on my back and pushed me forward. Ahead of me was Eddy. He was on the phone.

"Are we going to activate the emergency beacon?"

Eddy shook his head, no. He lifted the broken cellphone.

"Yes, sir," Eddy said. "We have her boyfriend. He was the last one to see your daughter and the people who took her."

I looked left and right as we reached the parking lot.

"Roger that, sir," Eddy said.

"So, what are we doing?"

"Let me think," he said as he got to the parking lot. Eddy stood at the edge of the doorway back into the mall. Instantly, I saw the Escalade making its way around the parked cars and toward us.

"Does she have her necklace on?"

I nodded to Eddy.

"Activate the beacon. We should be able to track her with that," Larissa said.

Eddy nodded. The three of us stood in the covered parking lot and Eddy fished out another cellphone. He looked at it and then me and finally Larissa.

As I was leaning on Larissa I blinked and felt like I was going to throw up. My stomach was doing flip flops. I had been kicked in the side and breathing was a little harder than normal.

"You okay kid?"

I looked at Larissa and shook my head. I had been punched and kicked and knocked unconscious. I was anything but okay.

Before I could answer the Escalade stopped in front of us. Eddy raised a finger into the air and then spoke.

"Okay, here's what we do," Eddy said, decisively. "You drive Cam's car back to the estate. We'll be on our way, soon. I need to figure out if Kyla has her secondary emergency beacon activated. If I activate it and the kidnappers notice, then they can disable it. Need to be able to triangulate her location. Just in case," Eddy said.

Eddy guided me to the SUV and helped me into the rear of the incredibly plush vehicle.

Once Eddy was in the SUV Lloyd looked at him curiously.

"What is our sit rep?"

Eddy did not answer immediately. He sat in the passenger seat looking at his secondary phone.

"We got a ping. So, we head to the ping first. If we find Cinderella, then we just turn around and head back to HQ. If we don't find her then we head back and regroup."

"Where to?"

"Looks like they're heading to the Strip," Eddy said. "I think we need to head back to the HQ," Eddy said. "Shit's hit the fan. We're in it now."

"Oh, shit," Lloyd said.

Oh shit, indeed I thought.

The SUV pushed out of the mall. The afternoon traffic was starting to build.

Lloyd drove toward Las Vegas.

They exited at the airport.

"This doesn't look good," Lloyd said.

The SUV circled the airport slowly.

"You don't think they hopped on a plane?"

"No," Eddy said. "Turn in here."

Lloyd turned into the airport parking lot. The SUV slid through the underground parking lot.

The SUV pulled up next to a Lincoln Continental.

Eddy climbed out of the SUV and examined the car. He opened the car doors and looked inside. He opened the rear of the car. Eddy examined the rear. He climbed back into the SUV with a facial expression that did not give anything away.

"What did you find?"

Eddy took a deep breath and lifted up Kyla's necklace.

"Okay, I need to call in some favors in Vegas," Eddy said, tossing his secondary phone on the Escalade dashboard. He fished out another phone and dialed.

"So, to the house?"

Eddy nodded and Lloyd pulled away from Lincoln and toward the exit of the airport parking lot. I watched as we inched along moving away from Las Vegas in bumper-to-bumper traffic. I looked out the window and watched as the city fell away and was gradually replaced with highways and desert sprawl. I thought about my car and Larissa driving it back to the Hudson mansion. I thought about Kyla and hoped she was all right. That thought clawed at me. It wasn't fleeting like the other thoughts. I was uncertain suddenly what was going to happen. The SUV swung onto a freeway exit and traffic loosened up. In a few minutes the SUV was on the road back to Henderson.

I leaned forward between the two seats in the front of the Escalade trying to see Lloyd and Eddy.

Eddy looked back, seeing me.

"So, how does this work?"

"What do you mean?"

"I mean, this stuff here," I said for clarity. "What happens next? How do we get Kyla back?"

"Well, that's two questions. First, the kidnappers snatched the target. They have to find some place to hide her, that's second. Then they are going to ask for a ransom, of some sort. Then they negotiate a drop-off point for the money. Then, if everything goes off without a hitch, they return the target."

I listened as the SUV made its way effortlessly back toward Foothill High School. Thinking about Foothill High School made me remember how I ended up with Kyla Hudson.

A month ago. Foothill High School is your typical high school. You know, freshmen, sophomores, juniors and seniors. There are nearly three thousand kids that go there. It was the place where genius and idiot walked down the same halls beside star athletes and valedictorians. In the halls of Foothill were potential political figures as well as business leaders, vagrants, dope dealers, porn stars, drug addicts and entrepreneurs and prostitutes.

There are all sorts of clubs and activities at Foothill, but the biggest the week after Kyla and I went to the movie was the gossip train. It seemed as soon as I arrived there were all these sly looks, smiles and nods from people I barely knew.

Okay, how does gossip work in high school?

It's not that complicated. It's like that game you play in elementary, telephone. Someone sees something or says something, and they tell the next person. The next person adds their little spice to it. Then they pass it on to their friend. It builds up a head of steam and all of a sudden half of the school finds out you are going out with, if not sleeping with, one of the hottest girls in Henderson.

I shrugged it off to just high school stupidity until I ran into Wes and Lyle. They found me at my locker preparing for my first period class. They were all smiles and laughs and then the questions began.

"So, how did you do it?" Wes asked.

"Do what?"

"Yeah, why did you keep it a secret from us?" Lyle asked.

"I didn't keep it a secret," I said. I tried to explain but Wes cut in.

"I thought we were your best friends?"

"What's that supposed to mean?"

"Did she tell you to keep it a secret?" Wes shook his head. "Be careful. She may be using you."

"Using me?"

Lyle placed a hand on my shoulder. He looked at me sympathetically.

I looked at the boy who loved belching more than anything in life other than playing video games and pizza.

"Were you embarrassed?"

Well, I thought about the question, but before I could answer Wes asked another question.

"Are you going out with her again?"

"Do you think that she likes you as much as you like her?"

It wasn't eight o'clock and I was being grilled by Wes and Lyle. The worst part of it was they didn't seem to want to hear my answers. They had all these questions that they needed to say to feel as if they were concerned, but I could tell their concern really was being nosy. It, the questioning, was a little disappointing. I expected the questions and the curiosity, that was natural. I wasn't prepared for the Hatorade they seemed to be drinking by the gallon that morning.

I knew I shouldn't have been surprised to find Wes and Lyle riding on the gossip train. Hell, I thought idly, I had jumped on many of the unsubstantiated gossip trains at Foothill when I was bored and needed something to talk about. I couldn't be mad at Wes or Lyle. They, like everyone at Foothill, were susceptible to gossip. In this case, they smelled blood in the water with a whiff of news about Kyla and me going to the movies over the weekend.

I have to admit it wasn't like we were keeping it a secret. I liked her. She liked me.

That Monday morning after listening to my friends, I closed my locker and headed to class without another word to Wes or Lyle.

In my English class sat Justice. He nodded seeing me. I sat down and waited for him to question me about Kyla, but his questions never came.

"You okay?"

"Yeah," I said with a nod.

English class began and I shook off the weirdness of Wes and Lyle. It was high school, I decided.

The first person to call me was Kyla. Well, she texted me during my English class.

We have to talk. Can you meet me in the 300 hall in five?

I texted Kyla back and raised my hand.

Mister Harper, our English teacher, was a big-eyed man with a bit of a beer belly. He usually dressed in polo shirts, jeans and comfortable shoes. We were reading a book for the class and before we began our reading, I waved my hand to get Mister Harper's attention.

"Yes, Weaver?"

"May I be excused?"

"Yes, you may," Harper smiled, having taught us all to speak properly.

"Pennington, you give young Weaver seven minutes to leave and return," Harper said to Margaret Pennington, the bathroom monitor.

Margaret Pennington was the boy's bathroom monitor for the week and as such was in charge of the digital clock for bathroom pass use. Pennington held the bathroom pass. When a student needed to leave the classroom for the bathroom Pennington was tasked with writing in the student's name and time of departure. asked to go to the bathroom. If the student came back early, he or she was marked down for the three total passes for the six weeks. If they came back later than scheduled, they would lose another pass. Going over bathroom passes was a mark against grades.

Thomas Daley was the girl's bathroom monitor. Harper did that purposefully. He did not want boys playing favorites with their friends.

Margaret Pennington smirked as I approached.

"Five minutes, starting now," she said, handing me the Boys bathroom pass.

I nodded and exited the classroom. Looking left and right and then I headed quickly to the 300 hallway.

"You hear the news?"

"No," I said.

"We're going out," Kyla said, her eyes bigger than usual.

"How's that news? I mean," I said with a shrug. "We went to the movies," I said.

"No, not the movies, Cam," Kyla said. "Someone saw us at the pizza parlor eating pizza and they have us going out."

I didn't get the point. I think I was a little denser than Kyla. In my head we went to the movies. That had happened. We had walked around and gone to the pizza parlor. I had gotten her a pizza slice with mushrooms on it. That had happened. What was the big deal?

I suppose I might have said the last thing out loud. It seemed like a big deal to Kyla.

"What's the big deal?" Kyla asked, her eyes growing bigger.

"You didn't want to go out with me?" I asked, with a small smile.

"No," Kyla said. She looked at me confused. "No. No. I didn't mean it like that," Kyla said, apologetically. "Of course, I wanted to go out with you. I just didn't want to have to deal with the stupidness of others being all in our business."

That I understood.

"Okay, check this out," I said, understanding. "I get that part. I like you Kyla," I said and waited for her to laugh or walk away or do something that would crush me. There was just her standing there near the bathroom looking at me and nodding for me to continue. "So, we're in high school. People like to be in other people's business. That's called being nosy. We don't have to let them get in our business." I paused. It was suddenly me and her and us against the others at Foothill. The realization was wild.

There was silence.

"You okay?" I asked.

"Yeah, I'm okay," Kyla said.

"So, welcome to high school and your first high school crush," I said.

"You crushing on me?" Kyla Hudson asked, her eyes no longer gigantic and a slight smile on her lips.

"Big time," I said.

Kyla smiled at that comment. I reached out and tried to touch her hand. She smiled and touched my shoulder.

"Okay, I'll see you later. I have to get back to class. Remember don't let them get to you," I said, with a chuckle. "See you at math."

"Okay," Kyla said as I smiled and found her hand in mine. I wanted to hug her but fought the desire for the moment. I released her hand and headed back to English class.

By lunch our relationship was high school level news. That meant, in my mind, that after a week of looks, stupid questions, haters and a bunch of more stupid looks from boys that had dreamed of talking to Kyla the whole thing would blow over. High school is built on the idea of the lack of long-term memory. The populous would glom onto an issue for a moment and after a week or two get bored and glom onto another issue. There was rarely any longevity of interest in things not important to everyone.

Kyla and my relationship status was just a blip on the high school radar because it was new. I might have been anybody with Kyla and they would have garnered the same amount of attention because she was a superstar. Her family had enough money and clout to send her anywhere and they chose to send her to Foothill. So, though I wanted to believe that people cared that I was going out with Kyla I knew they weren't. The few that cared about me were more curious about what I had done to get Kyla Hudson to go out with me.

That Monday, at lunch, Wes, Justice and Lyle told me that I was out of my league, but I didn't care. I liked Kyla. She was smart and funny and a little nerdy, like me. It didn't hurt that she was pretty, and I couldn't take my eyes off her.

"Man, you realize that you are going out with Kyla Hudson?" Lyle asked, unbelieving.

"The one and only Kyla Hudson?" Wes asked.

"She's Foothill's Beyonce," Justice said.

"Naw, she's Foothill's Blue Ivy," Lyle said with a smirk.

"Yeah, her parents are Henderson's Jay-Z and Beyonce," Wes said with a nod of his head.

"That's fine," I said, with a shrug. "I don't care. It doesn't mean anything to me. She's nice and smart and-- "

"She's easy on the eyes," Justice said with a sly smile.

The second half of Monday was just Monday, but on steroids. Whenever I went to class the kids who I barely said hello to wanted to talk to me. At first, I thought it was them being friendly. Then I realized they were trying to find out if what they had heard was true about Kyla and me.

By math class my head was swimming. It was good to see Kyla. She and I sat in our desks and watched as the class watched us.

"How are you doing?" I asked.

Kyla shook her head.

"That good?" I asked with a smile.

"You know I have never had to deal with this side of the gossip," Kyla said.

"It is definitely something," I said. "I think that it'll all blow over by the end of the week unless you kick me to the curb before then."

"What?" Kyla asked, confused.

"Well, everyone is all trying to figure out you and me. Right? They want to know what I did. They want to know what you did. Once they figure that out all the talk will die down," I said in a whisper as the teacher laid out the lesson for the day.

"You thought that all out?" Kyla Hudson asked, looking at me out of the corner of her eyes.

"I'm not just a pretty face," I said with a chuckle.

Tuesday was just like Monday only a day after. People who I didn't know came up to me and asked me random questions about Kyla. I usually didn't answer. Kyla and I had promised not to stoke the fire. We were only giving name, student ID number and the school address to everyone. If they wanted to know why we *didn't know ourselves. My favorite response was that God had gotten involved. Kyla and I used that anytime we wanted people to stop asking us questions. We weren't deeply religious, but we also knew that students would walk away with that answer.*

By Wednesday things seemed to be calming down.

Wes and Lyle were still being immature.

"Cam?"

"Yeah," I said to Wes at the lunch table.

"Why aren't you sitting with your girl?"

I didn't respond. There was no need. Things were still new between Kyla and me and I didn't want to move too fast. Kyla hadn't even introduced me to her best friends yet. So, instead of answering I just shook my head at Wes and ate my lunch.

Thursday things were not centered around Kyla or my relationship.

Chevon Butler, one of the football players, had been suspended from school and suddenly Foothill football was in jeopardy.

Friday, there was a junior varsity football game.

Saturday afternoon there was a varsity football game minus Chevon Butler. Foothill lost 24-7.

Sunday, I went to church. After church, I texted Kyla.

The second week of being Kyla Hudson's boyfriend was almost a normal week.

The second Monday, Kyla introduced me to a couple of her friends. There was Cindy and Morgan. I had seen them in the halls of Foothill but never thought to talk to them. Cindy was this sandy brown pouty model type with shoulder length, finger thick red and brown braids and perfectly arched eyebrows, almond shaped eyes and a runner's body. She looked like she should be playing volleyball or basketball, but she did not play any sports at Foothill.

Morgan was a chocolate beauty with a body that belonged to someone nineteen or twenty years old. She was sixteen and had a triangular face. Her Afro was usually divided into two hemispheres on her head, separated by her laser sharp parting. When I met Morgan, her Afro was braided and pulled back into a loose bun of braids.

The second Tuesday, Kyla and I sat in the gym with about sixty others and ate a bag of Takis and shared a soda. That was a big day for me. I didn't share anything with anyone.

The second Wednesday, Wes and Lyle were at the lunch table when I sat down. Wes had a devilish look on his face when I sat down with my lunch. I didn't even get to eat my cheeseburger when he leaned in and put a hand on my shoulder.

"Cam, can you do me a favor?"

I had my cheeseburger primed and ready to eat when Wes asked that question.

"What do you want?"

"Well, I figure that you have some kind of magic hoodoo going on to keep Blue Ivy interested in you and you might want to help out your best friend and tell me what you are doing or giving me some of the potion you are using."

Lyle, who was eating his fries, leaned in against my elbow, expecting me to say something.

I smiled. I looked at Wes and thought he was kidding.

"Don't hold out on us," Lyle said.

"I am not holding out," I said, still holding my burger in my hands and looking at Wes and Lyle. "I actually have no idea why things are going so well, but I was always taught that if it ain't broke don't fix it."

By the second Thursday things seemed to be returning to a semblance of normalcy then Kyla caught up with me in the hallway and looked like someone had run over her dog.

"Kyla, you have a dog?" I asked.

"What? No," she said.

With that out of the way, I looked at my troubled eleven-day girlfriend, concerned.

"You okay?"

"Cam," Kyla said, one day at school. "My mom and dad want to meet you."

"Like that?"

"Yeah, like that," Kyla said, all serious.

"What's wrong?"

"I think they want to scare you off," Kyla said, tremulously.

I reached out and touched her hand. Instantly, she was in my arms. I closed my eyes knowing what it looked like in the halls of Foothill High School. I opened my eyes and focused on Kyla. Students were streaming by, looking and pretending not to look. Teachers were standing in the hallway by their doors. There was a lot of chatter in the halls as students went to their classes. We were in the midst of it.

"Calm down, babe," I said. I wanted to laugh at calling her "babe," but I didn't. I took a breath. She didn't either. So, I continued on. "We got this. It's going to take a lot more to scare me off then having dinner with your parents."

Kyla was trembling.

"We got this."

"You sure?"

"I'm sure," I said.

We were supposed to have dinner that Saturday night, just me and Kyla and the family. Kyle Junior was planning on being there as well. It was going to be a royal inquisition.

The second Friday came, and Wes and Lyle were all jokes about my dinner date with the Hudson's. Justice had no words. He just shook his head and rolled his eyes at the idea of me meeting the Jay-Z and Beyonce of Henderson.

"Man, Cam, make sure your nails are clean," Wes said. "No one is going to be able to eat if your nails got dirt under them."

I checked my nails and Lyle and Wes laughed.

"How much you think they going to offer you?"

"Offer me?" I asked Lyle.

"Yeah, you know they probably going to try and cash you out to leave their little princess alone," Lyle said with a smirk. "Rich people are all about moving up the ladder. They probably got some Roderick Van Snooty Pants lined up for Kyla and you are in the way."

"Yeah, you know how they are," Wes said, with a nod. "They probably checked all your records and your background. They thinking about the future for their little baby. They can't just have anyone being Kyla's boyfriend."

I listened but tried not to think too much about what my friends, the pair of them, were talking about. In the back of my mind, I was thinking most of their talk was sour grapes. They had tried to talk to Kyla and none of them had gotten anywhere. So, though what they said made sense I didn't give it much credence.

I liked Kyla. Kyla liked me. At the moment, that was enough.

When school let out, I found Kyla and walked her to the front of the school where her SUV and guard were waiting. The same muscular guy who looked like he might be able to kick over a streetlight was standing by the SUV as Kyla, and I walked toward him.

"Missus Hudson," the guard said, opening the passenger side door and looking up and down the sidewalk for any threats in front of the high school.

Kyla stopped and turned and gave me a hug. Her arms wrapped around my neck and my arms held her around her waist. I closed my eyes and took in the heady smell of Kyla Hudson. She smelled like honey suckles and bubble gum. There was a hint of lemon twist that tickled my nose in the fragrance of Kyla that day.

"Call me when you get home," Kyla said into my ear as she held me. I nodded.

She released me and bounced to the SUV and into the rear seat. The guard closed the door and looked up and down the sidewalk for any threats.

The man, wearing sunglasses and an earpiece looked at me without emotion.

"Mister Weaver," the guard said with a slight nod and turned and climbed into the passenger seat next to the driver.

The SUV pulled away and headed toward the highlands.

I watched the SUV carrying Kyla drive away.

I rubbed my jaw and felt the aftereffects of being stomped by one of the bastards who kidnapped Kyla. With the constant reminder that I had been stomped out and Kyla kidnapped the idea of pride vanished. It was replaced with a feeling of frustration. Kyla was gone.

I watched as we passed all the local landmarks and then headed for the foothills where the select rich and famous lived. We were only five or ten minutes away from the high school, but as we drove it might as well have been five or ten million miles away from Highland Hills, where I lived. Ten or fifteen minutes above the high school was this area of Henderson that sat in the foothills and had incredible views of the desert in one direction and Lake Mead in another and Las Vegas in another.

<h1 style="text-align:center">Chapter 4.</h1>

Eddy and Lloyd went quiet five minutes before our arrival to the mansion. For five minutes I used the time to think over what I had gotten myself into. I knew I was fighting above of my weight class, but I liked Kyla. The craziest part, to me, was that Kyla Hudson really seemed to like me. For a crazy moment I felt like I was in one of those dreams where you are asleep and then you wake up and realize that you are still in the dream. I had all these doubts, but everyday Kyla would appear and smile at me or hug me or touch my hand and I knew she didn't smile, hug and touch any other boy's hand. It, her genuine like of me, was not lost on others.

One day, when I walked Kyla to the front of the school, and we waited for her car to pick her up she gave me a peck on the cheek before jumping into the car. The guards watched me as I stood on the curb. Kyla and her entourage drove away and there was this sudden emptiness in the gut of my stomach when the car turned and disappeared.

I spun on my heels and walked toward the school parking lot. It was still relatively early, and the parking lot was a hive of activity. Twenty plus cars were trying to snake their way out of the parking lot. Another twenty cars were still parked. There were two buses making their way through the parking lot.

It would take at least another fifteen minutes for the parking lot to clear, I figured. So, instead of heading to my car I turned and walked back into the school. I re-entered the emptying school and was greeted by the sound of people screaming and yelling and laughing and talking. Nothing unusual, I knew. Just kids' glad school was over. The hallways were emptying, and I walked to the middle of the hallway and for half a second thought about going to the library.

The library used to be my favorite spot at school. It held all these books and possibilities. I remembered the first person I met who remembered my name was the librarian. I walked to the end of the hall and paused at the library door. I reached out and was about to try the door when I heard someone call my name.

"Cam? What are you doing here afterschool?"

Justice was dressed in basketball shorts and T-shirt. On his feet were his basketball sneakers. Justice was playing on the Junior Varsity basketball team.

"I was just--" I said, not sure what I was going to say.

"You trying to check out a book or something?"

"Naw, I was just going to see what they had new in there," I said, feeling awkward.

Justice nodded.

"Basketball season start yet?"

"Naw, you know this is all pre-season stuff. The real games start in January and then the district games begin and then its three months of trying to make it to state."

I nodded.

"Hey, Cam, I wanted to tell you that I'm proud of you," Justice said. "I mean it. I know that we bust on you and all, but you and Kyla Hudson is big."

"How so?"

"I mean, she's legendary," Justice said.

I didn't respond.

"Don't let their money change you," Justice said. "I hear all sorts of horror stories about people getting all twisted trying to go after the money and forgetting why they got there."

I listened.

"You keep being you," Justice said with a curious smile.

"Hey, Justice, we about to warm up," a boy dressed in basketball shorts and T-shirt said from the top of the hallway. Behind him another basketball player was heading to the gym at the end of the hall.

"Talk to you later," Justice said and turned and sprinted toward the end of the hall and toward the boys.

Standing at the library, I turned and looked down the hall back toward the gym and then back to the library door. I closed my eyes and tried to think. There were all these thoughts in my head. There was this belief that I wasn't good enough for Kyla. There was this belief that the family was going to try and break me or intimidate me at their dinner. There was also the issue of them trying to buy me off. Then Justice had come out of nowhere and told me he was proud of me.

I smiled at the memory. It was nice to think how Justice was proud of me being with Kyla. It was a weird feeling, pride. It made me feel peaceful and sure.

I had survived two weeks of Foothill as the boyfriend of Kyla Hudson and prepared for the weekend and dinner with the Hudson's. For the craziest reason that last day before meeting Kyla's family played before me as Eddy and Lloyd weaved through the streets of Henderson and past the flatland housing development my mother and I lived in.

At the end of the day and week, when I drove home from Foothill and parked the Jetta, it was just me and my mom. I lived in Highland Hills. My mom and I had a house that was nice enough for us. It had three bedrooms and of course my mom had the biggest room. She used the third bedroom as her soon to be antique store office. She was trying to launch her own business in Henderson while working in Vegas as one of the managing supervisors for customer service at The Mirage.

My mom told me when we moved to Highland Hills that it was only a temporary move. Henderson was more affordable. She wanted to move closer to the Strip where she imagined she would open her antique store. I listened and after a year stopped waiting.

I liked living in Highland Hills. When things were said and done it was just me and my mom. It had always been that way. For as long as I could remember it was me and my mom.

My dad? When I try to remember my dad, it is like one of those faces you kind of recall the shape of and the eyes and maybe the voice but nothing more. He appeared when I was seven or eight. I saw him a few times on the streets of Henderson. I saw him a few times and then he moved out of state when I was ten or eleven and that was the last time, I remember seeing him.

My mom didn't talk about him. So, I didn't talk about him. All I could say about him was he was tall. He was dark. He didn't smile much. In my head, I came to realize that I didn't need him to validate me or make me feel like I was important.

I had my mom. We were doing well. We lived in a nice house in Henderson. It wasn't a mansion or anything, but I didn't care. All I cared about was that my mom and I were good. There was food in the refrigerator. We had electricity. I could watch cable if I wanted. The Internet was solid. What more was there?

The Friday I returned home from school, my mom, dressed in a floral blouse, jeans and tennis socks smiled at my return. She was on the far end of thirty and still this warm woman with freckles on her cheeks with an angular face that gave hints of her Native American lineage. She was sitting in front of a small café table she had decided we needed to accent the corner of the small kitchen. The café table was one of those small wrought iron outdoor tables that was usually in coffeehouses. She had found on the side of the road, coming home from the casino.

She was always finding treasures and putting them in storage. Her plan, according to her, was to build up an inventory of quality items then acquire a retail location and open competitively.

My mom loved rummage sales. If there was a yard sale around, she was usually there, looking for something. I loved her desire to find the undiscovered treasures hiding in a garage sale that would make her instantly wealthy or build her antique inventory.

Then, just two weeks ago, I got hooked up with Kyla Hudson. Me and mom became me and Kyla. Well, it seemed that way, initially.

I was in a hard like for Kyla. We talked all the time in those first seven days. What surprised me was that listening to Kyla talking about her day, her life, her parents or whatever never got boring. I just listened and imagined her telling me the story from her castle in the Foothills.

"Mom," I said seeing her sitting at the café table.

She looked up from a set of silver she was polishing lovingly. She had bought the silver set at a garage sale and knew was incredibly valuable. There was a tea tray, a tea kettle, teaspoons, tablespoons, forks and knives. My mom looked up and smiled at me. I was suddenly hesitant. My mom went back to her polishing of the tray she was concentrating on.

I stood there in the kitchen near the café table. I had planned on telling my mom about Kyla and that I was in a hard like of the Foothill High School Blue Ivy. I needed to tell her. I think I wanted to say the words and hear what my mom had to say in response, but I stumbled. For some reason, I lost my voice.

My mom looked up, concerned. "You got any plans for a Friday night?"

I scoffed. I thought about all I wanted to say. I might go and sit in the backyard. I might walk around the block. I might walk to Las Vegas, I thought. I usually didn't do very much on Fridays.

The difference was that this Friday Kyla was unavailable. I hadn't told my mom about Kyla Hudson. The person I told everything to for as long as I could remember I was now hesitant to talk about Kyla Hudson.

So, instead of mentioning Kyla or my hard like for Kyla or how I went to the movies with her I decided to tell my mom later, if things got serious. I mean, I was in high school. People went out and before the weekend they were broken up. I thought about all of this and decided that I was going to watch Netflix or YouTube and relax and hope that Kyla and my relationship lasted longer than a week. Of course, I didn't say any of that.

"I'm not sure," I said.

"Okay," my mother said and that was that.

I didn't bring up Kyla until I found out I was going to have dinner with her and her family.

My girl, Kyla Hudson, had been kidnapped. I had thought we were being robbed as the guy with crooked nose above a scruffy mustache and goatee had spoken showing off his gum dominated mouth and his diamond earring. The kidnapper with the gun and earring had been a distraction. He had stopped us in the parking lot and another guy pushed past me. I did not get a good look at the second guy wearing a Tennessee Titans hooded sweatshirt. But it was the third kidnapper who caught me by surprise. I had been stomped out. The one who punched me, tripped me and grabbed me and punched my lights out.

I was thinking about the kidnapper who had grabbed me and snarled just inches from me. He smelled like Axe cologne and onion rings. There was a sickly-sweet smell of marijuana under all the sweet and sour smell that assaulted me. He had thin brown eyes and thin lips below his broad nose. The puncher was also wearing braids.

"Park the car and meet us in the conference room," Eddy said, climbing out of the SUV. "He'll be here soon and want a debrief."

Lloyd nodded, silently.

When we parked, I was feeling a little better.

At the entryway were two guards.

Eddy and Larissa walked me to the living room. They stood on either side of me.

"Missus Hudson, here's Cam. He was the last one to see young Miss Hudson before the incident," Eddy said.

I stood next to Larissa and sort of felt like the odd man out.

"Thank you Eddy," Missus Angela Hudson said. "You can leave us. I believe Mister Hudson should be here shortly. He will want to talk to you."

"Yes, ma'am," Eddy said and bowed and exited with Larissa.

There were at least half a dozen people in the living room and main lobby area of the mansion.

The only person I knew, or recognized, was Kyla's mom, Missus Angela Hudson. She was dressed in a silk blouse and comfortable genie pants with ties at the bottom. On either side of her were seated two women I had never seen before.

On her right was a woman who looked a little like Missus Hudson, but with loose curly tendrils. Next to the curly haired woman, sitting on the arm of the couch, was a long-faced man with a broad nose and goatee, wearing a blue business suit, white collared shirt, tie and leather shoes.

On her left was a short haired woman with arched eyebrows, a sharp beak-like nose and full lips. She had a tennis bracelet on her wrist and a thick golden chain around her neck.

Beside the short-haired woman with the tennis bracelet, on the other side of the couch, was a sulking, square faced, thick shouldered man with a scruff of facial hair, wearing a Hawaiian shirt, jeans and basketball sneakers who was scowling at me as I stood looking at him. I didn't like the sulking man who looked like I was guilty before I said a word.

Lastly, in the living room, seated in a loveseat, sat an older brown woman with smoky eyes and a timeless look about her. She could have been thirty or sixty, as I looked at the smoothness of the woman's skin. There were no telltale wrinkles around her eyes or mouth to give away her actual age. Her straightened brownish hair was shoulder length and had loose curls throughout. Adding to her timelessness was her outfit was not too young or too old. She dressed in a bright floral spring dress and heels, in her earlobes hung diamond drop earrings and perched on her left hand was a big diamond ring.

"Cam," Missus Hudson said, serious and a little anxious. "This is my sister-in-law, Nicole. She's Kyla's aunt," Missus Hudson said.

She named everyone in the living room, and I tried to keep up, but the names fell in and out of my head after the introduction. I was still a bit rattled. It had been a memorable Thursday.

The man in the business suit, who was perched on the arm of the sofa, stood up and studied me. He was the only man dressed in a suit and tie. He looked like a banker or a car salesman.

The guy wearing the Hawaiian shirt just looked at me and scowled. He had a thick neck and broad shoulders that looked like they came from hours and hours in the gym. The wide-nosed and scowling big lipped Hawaiian shirt wearing man with a close-cropped haircut seemed annoyed to be there.

"So, what happened?" The sister-in-law asked. She looked up with her big eyes and tilted her head. I looked to Missus Hudson for guidance. Nicole, the sister-in-law, leaned forward to get a better look at me. In front of her, on the coffee table, was a glass of brown liquid.

"You think he was in on it?" The woman wearing a spotted dress asked.

I looked from Missus Hudson to the woman in the leopard inspired dress. Miss Billie seemed the correct name, but I wasn't sure. Maybe her name was Miss Millie?

"You in on it?"

I turned from the leopard inspired dress to the scowling Hawaiian shirt wearing man whose name seemed to be Xavier.

"How many kidnappers were there?" Lance or Rance, the business suit asked.

"Who was involved?" The tennis bracelet wearing woman asked, adding, "Were they black or white?"

I opened my mouth to answer only to hear another question.

"Where was the security?" Missus Hudson asked.

"How does this happen?" The business suit, asked with a shake of his head.

"Where were they when this happened?" The woman wearing a tennis bracelet asked.

I opened my mouth.

"They were at the mall," the Hawaiian shirt said.

"Why didn't the security protect her?"

"They lost her," the business suit, said.

"Why didn't they know where they were going?"

There was silence and I noticed everyone looking at me.

"She told me she needed a break," I said, unsure who had asked the question.

"See, Angela, I told you that you were smothering that girl," Missus Hudson's sister-in-law, Nicole said with a pout. She had her empty glass in her hand.

"Giving her too much room led to this," said the bird-like woman dressed in the spotted dress.

Missus Hudson stared down the bird-like woman.

"There has to be a balance," the older woman whose name I suddenly felt I needed to know said.

There was another pause. The man in the business suit placed a hand on his wife's shoulder. She looked at him briefly, dispassionately.

The woman wearing the leopard dress climbed to her feet and moved to the mantlepiece. She stopped against the mantle and posed. Above her was a gigantic painting of the Hudson immediate family. It was done in a contemporary style that mimicked a classic oil painting.

"Do you care about Kyla?"

I looked at Missus Hudson's sister-in-law who was looking at me with her cold brown eyes.

I didn't answer Missus Hudson's sister-in-law. I just sat there looking at the adults looking at me and thought how I this whole thing had come to this point.

Five weeks ago. We went to a movie at the local mall and for the life of me I could not tell you what we went to see. I mean I loved movies. I loved sitting in the theater and eating popcorn and drinking a soda and watching unlikely things happen to people pretending to be someone they were not. I just loved the whole movie experience. The only thing I disliked was waiting for the next big movie to come out. So, when I say I cannot recall the movie I took Kyla Hudson to see that is saying lots.

I have to admit I was all agog over Kyla. She was dressed that late afternoon in one of those basketball jersey dresses that are just incredibly eye catching on the right person. She was wearing a Golden State Warriors jersey dress for some reason and though I wasn't a fan I was a definite fan of Kyla Hudson that day.

She carried a cute little gold purse and was wearing blue and gold basketball sneakers. On her wrist was one of those smart watches that could do nearly anything. In her hand was her ever present cellphone.

We hugged and smiled, and I bought tickets to the movie. We walked into the lobby, and I paused. I could not believe that I was going to the movies with the hottest girl in Henderson. I knew there had to be hot girls everywhere, Henderson wasn't the epicenter of hotness by any stretch of the imagination, but I had never imagined me, Cameron Aloisius Weaver, with Kyla Hudson. It just didn't make sense.

I bought popcorn. I bought drinks. I was trying to be on my best behavior.

"Kyla, do you want anything else?"

"No," Kyla said with a chuckle. "I'm good."

We sat and I tried to play it cool sitting next to Kyla, but I was nervous. I didn't want to say anything stupid. I didn't want to spill the popcorn or drinks. So, I tried to breathe and pretend that she was just Wes or Justice or Lyle, but with those round cheeks, round nose and pouty, kissable lips kept reminding that she was the incredible Kyla Hudson.

"You okay?"

"Yeah," I said, realizing I was way too deep in thought.

We were about ten rows up from the screen in the center of the theater and waiting for the movie trailers to begin when I finally spoke.

"You are awfully quiet," Kyla said, nibbling at her popcorn.

"I—just—don't want to—say anything too stupid," I said with a shake of my head, my voice a little strained. "You know?"

"Relax," Kyla said, reaching out and putting her hand on mine. "I wouldn't have come if I didn't— if I didn't want to get to know you."

"Yeah, huh," I said. "I just never—I mean, I—I'm glad you did," I said, haltingly.

The movie began and there were about a dozen movie trailers before the movie. Again, I could not tell you what they were. All I know is Kyla was sitting next to smiling and eating popcorn in the dark and I was right next to her. She laughed and whispered to me during the movie. I usually did not like to have anyone talking to me during the movie, in general, but I didn't mind hearing Kyla's voice in my ear while the movie was going.

I did not say much when the movie started. I just sat back and enjoyed the ride. The movie watched me as I tried to play it cool and watch Kyla out of the corner of my eye. It took me half the movie to screw up the courage to put my hand on Kyla's in the dark.

I watched and waited for her to snatch her hand away or make a face or something or anything. She smiled. She turned and looked at me. I turned and we both smiled in the darkness of the theater.

As the movie was ending Kyla found her hand greasy from the popcorn. I offered her a paper napkin. Again, she smiled, and we both smiled in the intimacy of the dark theater where it seemed just her and me and the actors and actresses on screen.

When the movie ended, we went to the lobby.

"Did you like the movie?"

"Yeah, it was cool," I said, really talking about being with Kyla.

"I liked it too," Kyla said.

"Well, what do you want to do now?"

"Well," Kyla said, looking at her cellphone. "I have about an hour before I get picked up. So, you want to walk around the mall before I have to go home?"

I smiled as an answer.

Kyla and I walked around the mall and just window shopped and talked.

"You hungry?"

Kyla smiled.

We were near a pizza place.

"I'll get us a couple of slices," I said, silently calculating how much money I had already spent. I figured this situation was like Haley's Comet, a once in a lifetime kind of thing. I also figured might as well make it memorable. "What do you want?"

"Whatever," Kyla said with a laugh. "I like mushrooms."

"Got it," I said, walking into the busy pizza parlor. I walked to the counter and ordered. I looked back and found Kyla had followed behind. She was not next to me but hovering nearby. I smiled at her from the counter. She smiled back.

It was another tender moment that sealed my fate with Kyla. I was hooked. Hooked.

I paid for the pizza and gave Kyla her slice. We sat outside of the parlor and ate.

When it was close to Kyla being picked up, I walked her back to her pickup spot and waited.

"You don't have to wait," Kyla said.

"I know, but I want to," I said.

Kyla nodded and giggled. She leaned on me for the first time. I was a little surprised but did not give my surprise feeling away. I just laughed and shook my head.

Kyla looked at me, shocked.

"What?"

"You are a lot different than in school," Kyla said, with a timid smile.

"What did you expect me to show up with my backpack on and ask you questions about math," I said with a slight grin.

"No," Kyla said, shaking her head.

"You did," I said with a laugh.

Kyla continued to shake her head. She laughed too. Her laugh was like the sound of wind chimes. It was melodious.

She stopped laughing and looked at me with those big eyes of hers. Right then and there she could have said anything, and I would have said, "Yes."

Instead, I shrugged.

"You got a girlfriend Cam?"

"You asking?" I asked with a wide smile. "Or are you looking to fill a position?"

Kyla giggled and tried to punch me.

"If you trying to fill the position then I'll need to see your resume and contact three people for references," I said with a chuckle.

"Three?"

"Yeah, and it can't be your mom and dad," I said, joking. "They're not going to be honest about you."

"Why wouldn't they be honest?"

"Come on, you already know," I said.

"Okay, three people I need for references?"

"Right," I said.

"Can I use you?"

"Can you use me?"

"Yeah," she said. Before I could speak, she looked at me curiously. "Why not?" Kyla asked, suddenly naïve.

"I'm the one that needs to figure out things," I said, laughing. I looked at Kyla and shook my head. "Okay, let me flip this around, my beautiful movie date."

"You think I'm beautiful?" Kyla asked, adding, "You think this was a date?"

"Yes and yes," I said and shook my head. "This all started with you asking me if I had a girlfriend? Let me ask you a question. You seeing anyone right now?"

"I'm seeing you, right now," Kyla said, looking at me with those big brown eyes of hers.

"Okay, I'm seeing you, right now, too," I said.

There was a pause then.

Before I could say anything stupid or do anything a black SUV rolled up and out of the gigantic vehicle stepped a man in a dark suit, white collared shirt and tie. I noticed that the man had an earpiece in his ear. He was a dark brown man with short hair, a broad nose, wide mouth and bullish neck that sat above muscular shoulders and a powerfully built frame. The man's eyes were hidden behind sunglasses.

As soon as the man climbed out of the SUV he seemed to bristle with attention. I watched as he assessed the situation between Kyla and myself silently and the environment around us. Again, silently, he determined I was not a threat and opened the passenger rear door of the SUV for Kyla to enter.

"Miss Hudson," the man said, standing and watching up and down the sidewalk the three of us were standing on.

Kyla looked at the man and then back at me. I didn't move. I didn't know what was going on suddenly. Living in Henderson and close to Las Vegas I knew that there were people that had drivers and bodyguards, but I didn't know any of those people. Now, I did.

Instantly, I figured that the SUV was bulletproof and that the men were armed and wearing bulletproof vests. Making the wrong move could make me dead. It was a lot to take in after a movie and pizza with Kyla Hudson.

As I was silently freaking out about the idea of armed men, I didn't know near me, Kyla took two steps and hugged me. She wrapped her arms around my neck and pulled me in close. I hugged her back. I wanted to close my eyes, but I was afraid if I did the man at the SUV might walk up and twist my arm behind my back or at the very least punch me. So, I hugged Kyla and held onto her like she was life itself. She smelled like cotton candy and bubblegum, and I smiled at the heady combination.

Taking in Kyla's smell and feeling her breathing against my chest made me smile as the man with the sunglasses seemed anything but happy to watch me hugging her. I smiled at the fact that holding Kyla Hudson at that moment was the only reason I was not catching a beatdown.

Kyla released me and I stood there cherishing the moment.

"Call me," she said and ran to the car and climbed into the rear. The man closed the door of the SUV and slowly walked to his open door.

"What's your name?"

"Me? I'm Cam. Cameron Aloisius Weaver."

The man nodded and climbed into the SUV and drove off without another word.

I walked back to the parking lot and climbed into the Jetta I had been given the year before by my grandmother and drove home. It was a great day. I went to the movies with Kyla Hudson and not made a fool of myself. After the movie I had walked around with Kyla and gotten pizza and talked and not done anything stupid. I was pretty proud of myself as I drove home.

Missus Hudson placed a hand on my shoulder snapping me out of my memories and bringing me back to the present.

"Kyla and Cam are so cute together," Missus Hudson said, with a smile.

Her words made me smile. Smiling made me wince. The side of my face was sore. Instantly, I was reminded why I was in the Hudson mansion and being grilled by people I didn't know.

"Kyla is too young to be dating," said the woman in the leopard dress.

"How long you been involved with Kyla?"

"I don't like it," the business suit said.

"Why didn't you stop them?"

I looked at the guy in the Hawaiian shirt and wanted to release a few bombs, but I didn't. I looked at his gym muscles and looked away. I did not answer.

"You can see that he's a little nerdy," the Hawaiian shirt said, with a sneer.

Missus Hudson raised a hand and tried to stop the interrogation.

"This is what happens when you decide to send our angel to a public school to teach her a lesson," Missus Hudson's sister-in-law said with a shake of her head.

"Private schools don't guarantee safety or security, Nicole," her husband said.

Before they could begin another round of "blame-Cam-for-Kyla-getting-kidnapped" the conversation took a radical change.

"Do you think we should call the police?" Nicole asked.

"The police?" Xavier said, skeptically.

"The police? Seriously?" the older woman in the leopard-inspired dress said, mockingly.

"They can help," said Missus Hudson.

"Can they?" The Hawaiian shirt wearing man asked.

There was silence.

"Why are you thinking about calling the police?" The woman in the leopard dress asked.

"My daughter has been kidnapped," Angela Hudson said angrily, ready to tear off the old woman's head.

"Angela, I get it, but you know that they are not the best solution. I mean, do you think they can help?" The tennis bracelet asked.

"Fuck that. They aren't the smartest move," the Hawaiian shirt said, climbing to his feet. He was a stocky man in his thirties who was nursing a beer belly. "They don't like helping us."

"What do you mean?" The woman in the leopard dress asked.

"I mean, the police are supposed to know what to do," Nicole, the sister-in-law said.

"The police?" The gym muscle guy asked, with a shake of his head. "A lot of times they are jealous of what we got, because they know all that we had to go through just to get it."

"Yeah, the police," Nicole said, looking at the man in the Hawaiian shirt, annoyed.

"Maybe if we were a different hue," the sulking muscular man said, dismissively.

"We pay taxes," Angela Hudson said.

"Yeah, but they don't pay for our protection," the business suit said.

"I mean, that you get the police involved and suddenly things go to shit," the muscular man said.

"How?" Miss Hudson asked.

"Okay, you call the police," the business suit said, lifting his hands. "You got to know that they going to come up here armed and ready for war. Don't let them hear that you got your own security. They might arrest us, just because they don't want us protecting us."

"Anytime you have to call the police and tell them that there is a problem and then in the same breath tell them that you are black and six foot something," the Hawaiian shirt paused for a second. "You know they have an agenda."

"Right," said the bird beaked woman wearing the tennis bracelet.

"They don't care if we live or die," the leopard dressed woman said, with a shrug of her shoulders.

"If it ain't the Kardashians or Lady Gaga they don't give three shits about us," the Hawaiian shirted man said.

"What's my alternative?" Miss Hudson asked.

No one responded.

"The FBI?" Miss Hudson asked.

"They just as bad," the muscular man said, timidly.

"Then who?" Miss Hudson asked.

"Well, you know there's always Lou Bennett," Nicole said, looking at her manicured fingernails.

"Louis Bennett is not an option," Angela Hudson said.

"He is a criminal," the older woman said.

"He is certifiable," the Hawaiian shirt man said.

"He might be, but he gets the job done," the business suit said.

"If you put Louis Bennett on this, we get Kyla back no question," the woman in the leopard dress said.

Chapter 5.

Before Mister Hudson arrived, there was a flurry of activity and then the household fell silent when he arrived. If there was a question of who was in charge, before Mister Hudson's arrival it was answered when he drove through the gates. The tension was palpable as the guards snapped to attention and seemed more alert. All the personnel were standing at the ready when he walked through the front door accompanied by his assistant, Destiny Salter, and his personal lawyer, Curtis Beaumont.

Destiny Salter was a short, wide-hipped, big chested woman who looked like she never was alone by choice. The color of wood and with almond shaped eyes and full lips Kyle Hudson's assistant was incredibly attractive.

Behind Destiny Salter sauntered Curtis Beaumont. He was a handsome man who looked like he should be in one of those old-fashioned movies where people dressed wearing bow ties, starched white shirts, suspenders and jackets with pocket watches. That day, when Beaumont walked into the Hudson home, he was wearing eggshell white collared shirt, plaid jacket and red plaid trousers. He was carrying a butter soft leather briefcase. Curtis Beaumont looked deadly serious.

"That's my husband's personal assistant," Missus Hudson said to me. Destiny Salter was all of twenty-two when she walked into the Hudson mansion dressed in a white blouse, blue jeans and comfortable leather shoes. In her hand was a notebook tablet. On her back was a backpack that looked like a utility pack more than rucksack. There were two bottle waters visible in the side pockets. Hanging from one of the clips was a travel size bottle of hand sanitizer. There were several markers visible in a see-through pocket. Her hair was pulled back into a ball of black curls on the top of her head.

"She's just a year out of UNLV," Missus Hudson's sister-in-law said with a sneer. "She wants to be the next big thing in real estate," Nicole added. "So, she has been sniffing around us for at least two years. She lives in Henderson and was an intern for a year?" Nicole asked her sister-in-law.

"Yeah, Kyle liked her determination. He hired her as an assistant last year," Missus Hudson said. "Her day starts early and goes late every day. Kyle has her on 24-hour call, just in case there's some real estate emergency," she said with a shake of her head.

"Are there ever real estate emergencies?"

"Not that I know of," Missus Hudson said with a tiny smile. "It's just a control thing for him."

"That's definitely my brother," Nicole said with a grin.

"You ever worry about Kyle having wandering eyes?"

Missus Hudson looked at the bird beaked woman and wrinkled her lips instead of speaking.

"I mean, she's that young and impressionable assistant," the bird beaked woman said, struggling.

"You see all this," Missus Hudson said gesturing to her curvaceous figure and smiled. "My man is definitely satisfied when he leaves the house."

"Don't get me wrong Angela," the bird beaked woman said with an awkward smile. "I was just curious."

"Kyle Hudson is all about his business and building our empire," Angela Hudson said with a smirk.

"Yeah, he ain't got that wandering eye in him," Nicole said with a small smile. "You know I know my brother," she said with a chuckle.

"Yeah, I do," Angela Hudson said.

Once Mister Hudson stepped into the house everyone answered to him. He was dressed in a lightweight brown suit, white collared shirt and lace up leather shoes when he walked into the house. Kyle Hudson, seeing everyone gathered in the living room, paused long enough to scan all those gathered and stop on Cameron.

"Let's go to the conference room," Kyle Hudson said turning on his heels and walking to the glassed-in room above the living room. Closely behind him followed Destiny Salter and Curtis Beaumont.

The group in the living room climbed to their feet. They slowly made their way to the glassed-in room.

"Cam, come sit next to me," Missus Hudson said, patting the space beside her at the conference table.

I moved robotically toward Missus Hudson under the unblinking eyes of all those gathered. I concentrated on Missus Hudson. I sat next to her and smiled. She seemed genuine in her affection toward me.

"So, tell me what happened," Mister Hudson said to no one in particular. Mister Hudson was sitting at the head of the table dressed in his suit and pocket square.

Eddy and Larissa, the two bodyguards, were there. Eddy was standing at the foot of the conference table with Larissa. Eddy lowered his eyes like a beaten dog.

Eddy began his story.

"We went to pick up your daughter at our scheduled time and she was not at the pick-up location."

Kyle Hudson steepled his fingers in front of him. Behind him Destiny Salter sat to his left. Curtis Beaumont sat to his right. Missus Hudson was on his right hand. I was next to her. Next to me, to my left, was the older woman with the gigantic diamond on her finger. On the far side of her sat Xavier.

"What did you do then?"

"We discovered she had decided to go to the mall with Cameron maybe fifteen minutes after we arrived for pick-up. Larissa was sent to search for Kyla, Miss Hudson. We activated the primary tracker and headed to the mall. We drove to the mall and found her phone, but it was broken."

"Yes, yes, I know all this," Kyle Hudson said, annoyed and impatient.

"Well, we were met by the mall security and told of young Cameron being held in the security office."

"I don't care about any of that," Mister Hudson said, steepling his fingers in front of his piercing dark eyes.

"We activated the secondary emergency beacon once we learned that Cam had been beaten and seen the kidnappers. Young Cameron was a little beaten up, but we figured he was our best chance of identifying any of the kidnappers. So, we sent Larissa back with Cam's car. We went to retrieve the secondary beacon with hopes of locating Miss Hudson. The pursuit proved fruitless. We found the car, but her necklace was removed and left in the car."

"Eddy, do you have any leads? Clues? Inclinations? Anything that is going to get my daughter back?" Mister Hudson asked.

"Well, sir, we know that Cam saw the three men," Eddy said.

In the middle of the sentence in walked a woman who looked like she was part Rihanna and part Alicia Keys and over six foot tall and two dark men. The woman had her short tar black hair plastered to her head like Josephine Baker and was the tallest of the three and gave off an athletic confidence. Looking at her there was a familiarity about her that I could not place. She was the color of cashews and had a neatly trimmed short and shaved curly Afro. The beauty had a broad nose and dark, piercing green eyes. The distinctive feature about her was her lack of jewelry. She wore no earrings, necklaces or accoutrements. She was long limbed and looked like she might have played basketball a long time ago. Her hands were incredibly large. Dressed in a white button-down shirt, untucked, jeans and basketball sneakers she looked like she might have been thirty years old.

Next to the basketball player was a six-foot-two-inch tall muscular and dark man wearing Clark Kent glasses and dressed in blue hooded sweatshirt, jeans and basketball sneakers. I watched as he entered the room, and the lenses of his glasses went from dark to clear as he first entered the conference room. It wasn't until he was beside Mister Hudson that his glasses were clear enough to reveal his light brown eyes. He had a semi-permanent smirk on his sand-colored face. He had a tight fade that rested above his small ears and included a laser etched part on the left side of his head. The nameless man looked like he might be able to rip off his sweatshirt and pose for a bodybuilding magazine. He had a round nose and thin mouth with a scar on his chin.

The third man, the last man to enter the Hudson conference room, was the combination of the two he followed. Not too tall. Not too muscular. The third stranger was just six foot tall and maybe two hundred pounds, if that. He was clean shaven, angular featured and possessed dark, brooding eyes. Through his left eyebrow was a visible scar. He entered the conference room dressed in a collared shirt, unbuttoned, a white T-shirt, blue jeans and unlike the others, dress boots. Around his neck was a gold chain and a medallion with a rhino's head on it.

"Just in time," Mister Hudson said with a laugh. He greeted the three like old friends, and they looked around and sat at the conference table, casually.

Everyone at the table seemed to know the three except me.

"You were about to tell us what the next steps are for retrieving my daughter," Mister Hudson said reclaiming his position at the head of the table and hiding behind his steepled fingers. The three new guests stood and listened near the only door in and out of the conference room.

"Well, sir," Eddy said, fumbling. "We did a preliminary search but came up with nothing. Our options are limited. Of course, we could pursue the Las Vegas and Henderson police and seek their assistance. If you want to push it up the chain, then I might be able to contact the feds. You just have to let me know what you think is the best approach as you have sensitive matters in your businesses and we are aware of your desire for privacy."

Mister Hudson listened behind his steepled fingers.

"What is the timeframe?"

"Well, sir, the sooner the better. We know there will be a ransom note coming sooner than later." Eddy paused. "So, if you can give us some direction before things ramp up it would be appreciated."

Hudson nodded.

"Is there anything else?"

"No, sir," Eddy said. "We just have to wait for how you want to proceed."

Mister Hudson looked at the clean-shaven man with the dark, brooding eyes. I could not take my eyes off the long face and the scar that ran through his left eyebrow and the finger thick gold chain and medallion with a rhino on it.

The stranger leaned in and whispered something to Mister Hudson. Hudson looked at his security guard and nodded. He then looked at me.

"One more question Eddy," Hudson said. "Had you or Lloyd seen any cars following you?"

"No, nothing I can think of," Eddy said.

The stranger looked at the tall woman and silently made a signal to her. She nodded and turned to the muscular man next to her. He nodded and walked out of the room without word. I watched as the trio seemed to be incredibly comfortable with one another.

The man with the rhino medallion whispered something else in Mister Hudson's ear and Hudson nodded.

"Eddy? How did you find Cameron?"

"We turned on the GPS sir," Eddy said, lowering his eyes.

"Does Kyla have any other emergency beacons?"

"No, sir," Eddy said.

"You can go Eddy," Hudson said. "Don't leave the property." Hudson looked up and saw Larissa.

"Larissa, you have anything to add?"

"No, sir," she said.

"You can go too," Hudson said.

Eddy and Larissa exited the conference room.

Everyone watched as the two security members left.

I looked too and when I looked back found Mister Hudson looking at me.

"Cameron? Is what Eddy told us correct?"

I nodded.

"Did you have a chance to do anything?"

I thought about what Mister Hudson was asking. Could I have stopped the three kidnappers from snatching his daughter? I tried to replay what had happened and at the end the ambush was so unexpected and there was a guy with a gun who froze Kyla and me right before the second guy grabbed Kyla. Maybe, just maybe, I could have done something then, but I thought the guy might shoot me or Kyla. Those two people, the one with the gun and the one that grabbed Kyla took all my attention. I didn't even know there was a third guy until he punched me.

I looked at Mister Hudson and shook my head.

"Things happened so fast, sir," I said, finally.

Mister Hudson nodded.

He looked to the two nameless strangers and paused.

The clean-shaven man leaned over to Mister Hudson and whispered something into his ear.

Mister Hudson climbed to his feet and Destiny Salter mirrored her boss's actions and walked out of the conference room.

The two men talked briefly outside.

Destiny Salter walked back in and looked around the conference table.

"Cameron, you need to come with us," Destiny Salter said. "Mister Hudson needs Miss Taylor and Mister Hill as well," the assistant said and stepped back into the hallway.

I looked around the conference room as the tall woman basketball player and the thickly built man wearing the Clark Kent glasses walked out of the conference room and began following Mister Hudson and the other man. I wasn't sure if I should leave the conference room. In the conference room was Missus Hudson. She was the only one that seemed friendly in the family toward me, other than Kyla.

"Cam, you go along with Kyle and tell them whatever they need to know. I'll call your mom and let her know you are here," Missus Hudson said with a smile. The rest of the family sat at the conference table unmoving. "Everyone stay seated," Missus Hudson said.

I slowly climbed to my feet and looked in the direction where Mister Hudson and the others were headed. I looked back at Missus Hudson. She nodded and smiled.

I walked out of the conference room and into the hallway where Destiny Salter waited.

"Cameron?"

"Yes," I said, looking at the woman that was a little shorter than me.

"Come along," Destiny Salter said, walking toward the western side of the mansion.

I walked in step with Mister Hudson's assistant and tried to figure out what I had gotten myself into.

"You're Mister Hudson's assistant?"

"Yes," Destiny Salter said, with a little smile.

"Who is that?"

I pointed to the man next to Mister Hudson.

"That's Louis Bennett," Destiny Salter said. "He's the finder of lost things."

Chapter 6

Louis Bennett seemed so nonchalant and at ease with Mister Hudson in the exercise room when I arrived. He seemed friendly and incredibly loose to me with the always business-oriented father of Kyla Hudson. Dressed in his unbuttoned collared shirt he was a distinct contrast to the business professional Mister Hudson. Louis Bennett was dressed casually, but everything was immaculately put together. His unbuttoned collared shirt was ironed and seemed wrinkle resistant. His blue jeans were the only things that showed a designed wear. This bald man with a brooding intensity that oozed from his dark eyes stood at arm's length from Mister Hudson. His clean-shaven look gave him the impression of someone well-kept and friendly as I walked cautiously into the exercise room.

The finder of lost things watched me silently. The lawyer was sitting beside Mister Hudson. The big armed man wearing the hooded sweatshirt, who was seated on one of the exercise benches, nodded and smiled.

"You want a water or something?" Destiny asked.

I looked at the big boned woman and nodded. Destiny pulled one of the bottled waters from her backpack and handed me a drink. She walked and sat on a weight bench near Mister Hudson. He rubbed at his temple. I followed Destiny Salter and took in the leader of the trio as I sat down near Destiny Salter.

Louis Bennett, the finder of lost things, looked at me with his dark eyes and the idea of him being friendly evaporated. He seemed incredibly intense. He looked like he was looking through me and thinking of quantum physics or something.

"So, how did you and Kyla ditch Eddy and the team?" Mister Hudson asked.

I swallowed, finding every adult looking at me. I knew that Mister Hudson was going to ask that question. He had to. I had been playing with it ever since I had been driven to the gates of their home. I took a deep breath and answered. I told Mister Hudson about Kyla telling me she was feeling a little suffocated. I also told him about Kyla and I leaving the campus an hour before school let out.

"I thought the campus was closed until school dismissal?" Curtis Beaumont asked.

"Well, sir, I think we left at the point when buses were arriving and the security was focused on them," I said to Mister Hudson's lawyer.

The lawyer nodded and looked to Mister Hudson.

Mister Hudson sat on the nearest bench and nodded.

"What happened when you and Kyla ditched Eddy?" Mister Hudson asked.

"Well, sir, we went to the mall." I paused. "I told her it was a bad idea," I said, feeling everyone's eyes on me. I swallowed. My throat was suddenly dry. I looked at the bottle of water. I twisted it open and looked at the adults looking at me.

"I know my daughter," Mister Hudson said. "Once she gets something in her head it takes God and His angels to remove it. So, you don't have to beat yourself up about that." He paused and looked at me with a small smile on his face.

"You look like someone already took care of that already," Curtis Beaumont said, with a grin. He chuckled.

I must have grimaced.

"You got your ass whooped," Mister Hudson's lawyer said.

I did not respond. I didn't dislike many people. I tried to be nonjudgmental, in general, about people, but I did not like Mister Hudson's snarky lawyer.

Mister Hudson gritted his teeth. He looked at his lawyer with a sidelong look. The lawyer smirked and nodded.

"Sorry, Cameron about that," Mister Hudson said, looking at his lawyer annoyed. "So, why did you guys go to the mall?

I sipped at my water. I sipped and tried to remain calm.

"She wanted to," I said as an explanation.

"She wanted to?" Mister Hudson repeated. He smiled and added, "The mall?"

"Yes sir," I said.

Mister Hudson nodded.

"Hud, let me ask a few questions," Louis Bennett said, in a low tone.

Mister Hudson nodded.

"Cameron, my name is Louis Bennett," the man with the scar running through his left eyebrow said, with a gravelly voice. "Were you caught off guard?"

I didn't speak. I just looked at the man in the collared shirt and nodded.

"How many snatched Kyla?"

"Three."

"Were they armed?" Louis Bennett asked.

"One was," I said. "He had a gun."

"The others were unarmed?" Louis Bennett asked but did not wait for me to reply.

I nodded, thinking.

Louis Bennett looked at the tall woman and the muscular man. He seemed to already be thinking about something else. Bennett looked at the muscular man. The man looked at Bennett alert.

The man stood up straight. "Tip is on the way to the Galleria," the man said. "He should be getting the video."

Louis Bennett nodded. He turned to Mister Hudson.

"We sent Tip there after you called me," Louis Bennett said to Mister Hudson.

Louis Bennett looked back at me and paused, thinking.

"Cameron, what time did you and Kyla get to the mall?"

"I think a little before three," I said, thinking. "We were there before three because the first phone call came after we left Build-A-Bear."

"Build-A-Bear?"

"Yeah, she wanted to go there," I said to Mister Hudson.

"How long were you there?" Louis Bennett asked.

"At Build-A-Bear?" I asked.

"No," Bennett said. "At the mall."

"I think we were leaving a little after five when they grabbed Kyla," I said, recalling the man with the gun stopping us in the parking lot.

"And you said there were three men?"

"Yes, sir," I said.

"Three? One to distract. One to control you. One to take Kyla," Louis Bennett said, thinking

"Sounds like these guys weren't amateurs," the basketball player said.

No one disagreed.

"That means they aren't cheap," the musclebound man in the hoody said.

"Hud, what's going on?"

Mister Hudson did not answer.

"I do not advise you to say anything," said the lawyer.

"This ain't a courtroom, counsellor," said the muscular man in the hoody.

The lawyer looked at the musclebound man and did not respond.

"Who would want to do this, Hud?" Bennett asked and looked at Mister Hudson.

Mister Hudson frowned. He climbed to his feet. He seemed surprisingly agitated. He turned on his heels and walked to the far side of the exercise room silently. Mister Hudson turned and raised a hand to stop his assistant from following.

Destiny Salter climbed to her feet but hesitated.

Louis Bennett walked to Mister Hudson's side. Mister Hudson seemed angry. Louis Bennett placed a hand on Mister Hudson's shoulder. The two talked in hushed tones. I strained to hear but the pair were too far away to discern what they said.

The conversation was not long but animated. I studied the others in the exercise room. Destiny Salter pulled out her phone and typed a few messages. The lawyer checked his watch. The tall woman with the notebook computer sat at a bench and stretched her long legs out in front of her. The musclebound man sat across from the tall woman and laid on the bench with his arms at his side.

Destiny Salter sat and then stood. She was a ball of energy. She watched the conversation between Bennett and her boss from near me.

I was just getting up the courage to ask a question when Louis Bennett, the finder of lost things, broke away from Mister Hudson and crossed back to the main area of the exercise room.

"Who is Wander Brett?"

The lawyer frowned and looked down at his shoes instead of answering.

Louis Bennett stood in front of the lawyer.

The lawyer looked up, thinking.

"Brett is a low-level but hungry realtor. He made a bunch of threats this year claiming Mister Hudson has been painting outside of the lines," the lawyer said, parsing his words.

"Does he have money to finance something like this?"

Curtis Beaumont looked at Bennett quietly. He nodded.

"Are there others?"

The lawyer opened and closed his mouth without a word.

"Mister Hudson is one of the biggest black realtors around. Becoming the biggest means that others aren't. That's simple. So, there are several rivals trying to knock Mister Hudson off the top," Curtis Beaumont said. "The three biggest rivals are David Charlotte, Brewer Collins and probably Cyril Paulson."

Bennett took all the information in from the lawyer.

"Who do you think has the balls to do this?"

"Probably Charlotte or Brewer Collins," Beaumont said.

"Not Brett?"

"I think he's the dog behind the fence, barking," the lawyer said.

"All bark and no bite," Bennett said, with a nod.

The lawyer nodded.

"Why the others?"

"They aren't as powerful as Mister Hudson, but they are the ones closest in terms of competition," Beaumont said. "They have the most to gain if Mister Hudson is off his game."

Bennett nodded.

"They ever threaten Hudson?"

"This is Henderson. There are a lot of threats," Beaumont said. "I get paid a lot of coin just to issue restraining orders and cease and desist orders."

Bennett grinned at the lawyer's words. "Yeah, I get that," Bennett said. He nodded, thinking. "Anybody else?"

"Well, there is always the Guidos in Vegas," Beaumont said, touching his index finger to his nose and pushing it to the left slightly. "They still have their fingers in all the pots in Vegas. Henderson is no different."

"Great," Louis Bennett said. "You got anybody that jumps to the head of the get Kyle Hudson list?"

"Like I said, there's Charlotte, Brewer Collins, Wander and Cyril Paulson." Curtis Beaumont paused. "There's always a few low-level wannabe Vegas realtors trying to branch out here. They are trouble, but I don't think they have the Cahoones to do something like this."

Louis Bennett twisted his lips into a half grin and frown. He nodded to the lawyer. He turned away from the lawyer and to the two he had come with him.

"Okay, that's it for me, for now," Louis Bennett said sitting down on the bench again. "Shay, take Cameron and work your magic." Louis Bennett pointed to the far side of the exercise room. He gestured and the tall girl walked toward me.

She gestured and continued to walk toward a corner of the exercise room. I followed behind her slowly. By the time I reached her, she had opened her notebook computer and started it up.

"Need you to describe who you saw," the tall woman said.

I stood there thinking of what that meant.

"Okay, need you to think now and try and remember what the three guys looked like," the tall and tone woman said, walking behind me. She stopped briefly and smiled.

"You can call me Shay," she said with a smile. The tall woman was attractive, but her physical features were completely out of proportion. Her big eyes reminded me of deer eyes. They were so big and shiny. She also had extremely long eyelashes. "All right, Cam. We need a description of the guys. Can you describe the guy with the gun," the woman said, looking directly at me.

"What?" I asked. "I thought you were going to contact the police or the FBI," I said, confused.

Bennett, not that far away, turned and narrowed his eyes. He climbed off the bench and walked to Shay's side. I was a little surprised to find Mister Bennett back so soon.

"The police?" Bennett asked, with a frown. "How long have you been on this earth? You ain't brand new? But you acting like you are," Bennett said as if the words were poisonous. "The police aren't protecting and serving *us*. They have their own agenda. So, we cannot rely on them. We can't trust them."

"But what about the FBI?" I asked, echoing the questions from earlier.

"We don't have time for jokes, kid," Bennett said through gritted teeth. He seemed angry for some reason.

I wasn't joking. I didn't speak, but it seemed as if Bennett read something on my face.

"They aren't that much better than the police," Bennett said. "Here's how it works. If you have to hurry up and wait for help, then that isn't really help. It's like getting raped twice by the same sonuvabitch, you ask me," Bennett paused. "I mean, we need help and when we ask for it, they never believe us because we aren't them. They more than likely will interrogate us and try and blame us before believing us. They don't' believe *us* because we don't look like them. So, we fight to be seen as victims while being victimized. It's a fucked-up situation. So, I don't trust them. It's a two-way street and both are going in the opposite direction."

"But what if the police want to help?"

"See, the difference between me and you kid, and everyone else here, is that we don't work in a world of hypotheticals. What ifs are the ice cream castles of dreams. The problem with your what if belief in the police and this government is that they were not created to help us. They want to arrest us. They want to jail us. They want to make us work for them. But they don't want to help us. They only investigate us to hunt us for their own twisted desire to prove they are better than us," Louis Bennett paused. "They don't have any desire to help us out of the goodness of their hearts."

"They don't have hearts," Shay said, agreeing with Bennett.

I looked at the tall and attractive woman skeptically. What she said was nonsense. Everyone has a heart.

"They are the new slave catchers," the musclebound man wearing the hoody said.

I shook my head at the musclebound man. Slavery was over.

"You want to help us find Kyla?" Louis Bennett asked.

"Of course," I said to Bennett.

"Then help," Bennett said.

"What can I do?" I asked.

"Help us find the guys that snatched her," Bennett said.

Find them? I wasn't a detective. I wasn't some private eye. I was just some sixteen-year-old kid who listened to Kyla Hudson and got sucker punched while at the mall and woke up to find my new girlfriend snatched. I was thinking all this, and the expression must have been visible on my face.

"Is there a problem, kid? Do you have somewhere to be right now?"

"No," I said, a little embarrassed.

"Good. Now describe the guy with the gun," Louis Bennett said as evenly as possible.

I closed my mouth before speaking.

"There were three men," the clean-shaven Louis Bennett said, without any expression in his voice. "Describe the one with the gun."

Louis Bennett walked away, leaving me with the tall woman. I watched as Louis Bennett sat next to the musclebound man.

Louis Bennett was sitting on the end of a bench, calmly and as matter-of-factly as imaginable.

"Can you describe the guy with the gun?"

The basketball player sat on one of the workout benches with her notebook computer and a graphic pencil.

I tried to think about the whole incident. The guy had appeared, and he was wearing a Las Vegas Knights hockey jersey. He was white. He had blonde hair. He had big eyes. I recalled that he was trying to squint but his eyes were really big and icy blue. His skin was pebbly. It looked rough, like sandpaper. He had a thin mustache above his thin lips. When he spoke, I think he had a gold tooth in the right side of his mouth.

He was right-handed. He had a hand tattoo on the back of both of his hands. I tried to recall the strange tattoo. I thought it was an "M."

"Okay, that was good kid," Shay said. "Anything else?" Shay thought. "Any jewelry?"

"Think he was wearing a thick gold chain with one of those pistol medallions dangling from it."

"Okay," Shay said, give me a few minutes and you tell me if I'm close," Shay said.

I climbed to my feet and walked to the opposite side of the exercise room.

"Now, what?"

"When you went to the mall do you remember seeing those guys before they jumped you?" Louis Bennett asked.

"No," I said. In all the time that I had been taken from the mall by Eddy and Larissa I had been replaying everything that had happened. I tried to imagine if I had seen any of those guys in the mall, but I had been Kyla focused.

"Did you see the car they were driving?"

"Well," I said, with a little hesitation. I tried to think if Eddy had told Mister Hudson about tracking the car to the Las Vegas airport.

"I mean, before Eddy and you drove to the airport," Bennett said.

"No, sorry," I said.

"I have a couple more questions, while we wait," Mister Hudson said.

"Shoot," I said, with a mild headache coming on from so much concentration and remembering.

"Okay," Mister Hudson said. "You and Kyla haven't been playing the grown up together? Have you?"

I frowned at Kyla's father. He was so confusing. Instantly, right or wrong, I disliked him. Did he care about Kyla? Did he love her? I know I shouldn't have thought this, but I couldn't help it.

Here we were in his house trying to find the guys that had kidnapped his daughter and he was trying to figure out if I had gotten passed Kyla gates.

I wanted to be angry. I wanted to scream. Instead, I just sat there and looked at Mister Hudson, Louis Bennett, Destiny Salter, the lawyer and the musclebound guy in the background and steamed.

"Cam, I asked you a question," Mister Hudson said.

I took a breath. I looked at Mister Hudson and the adults looking at me suddenly.

"I know, sir, but I don't think I'm going to answer your question," I said.

The response seemed to surprise Mister Hudson and the others near him.

Mister Hudson narrowed his eyes and tightened his lips as if he was fighting himself not to speak. Hudson took a deep breath and started to climb to his feet and toward me.

Louis Bennett placed a hand on Mister Hudson's shoulder, stopping him from getting to his feet or moving toward me.

"What you expect, Hud? Kid ain't stupid enough to come right out and say he was doing the grown up with your daughter," Bennett said with a smile.

Mister Hudson looked at Louis Bennett and then back at me angrily like he wanted to strangle me. I stood my ground. With everyone around me I didn't think that Mister Hudson was going to go all psychotic right then.

The tall woman appeared by Louis Bennett. The two looked at the notebook screen. Mister Hudson looked and then she showed it to me. Shay had combined all the details I had offered. When she showed me the composite of details that made up the white gunman.

There were a few things to correct. His nose was too broad. His eyes were too small. I pointed out that his lips were thinner.

A few minutes later she had the general idea of the gunman.

"Now, try to describe the guy that punched you?"

The guy that punched me was a snake. He was wearing an oversized watch and a thick chain around his neck. He had a crooked nose and a nose ring and a U-shaped face. The guy was dark brown and of average build.

He had a mustache, chipmunk cheeks and a gapped tooth grin. He smelled of weed. He had one of those tattoos that began behind his ear and snaked toward his shoulder. The tattoo looked a little like the tail of a lizard.

The guy who punched me was wearing a baseball jersey and jeans. On his feet were a pair of Doc Marten boots. I noticed that when he stomped me to sleep.

The tall woman reappeared. She showed me the composite. It was a good beginning, I thought.

"What did I miss?"

A few more details and a few more attempts got me close to the man that held the gun on Kyla. A diamond shaped face solidified the impression of the man who had stopped us in the Galleria parking lot.

The tall basketball player climbed to her feet and handed her notebook to Bennett. The two looked at each other and nodded. Then Bennett looked at me.

"Is this the guy?"

I looked at a composite of the features I had detailed. It wasn't the guy, exactly but most of the parts of him were there. I nodded, impressed with the basketball players skills on computer.

"Got it," Bennett said. "Okay, see if you can get the guy that sucker punched you."

The tall woman was an artist and in a few minutes after my initial description she showed me the composite of the guy who had cold cocked me. Having seen how the artist worked I began where we ended and worked backwards to get faster results. It took us a little over an hour to finish both computer-generated sketches.

The man that had punched me with no warning looked at me from the computer screen of the basketball computer artist and I was satisfied that both images were as good as I could get unless I saw them on the street and took a picture.

"What do you remember about the third guy?"

I didn't remember very much about the third guy. I tried to think if there were any details that might help.

After Shay was done with the sketch based on my spotty work, I walked away from her and her notebook computer.

"Don't think I helped that much on the last one," I said to Louis Bennett and the musclebound man.

"You don't remember anything?"

"He just sort of showed up. The third guy just appeared and disappeared so quickly I didn't get a good look at him," I said, sadly.

The third guy was bigger than both the other guys. He was maybe a foot taller than Kyla. So, maybe six foot one or two inches tall. He was wearing a baseball cap. I tried to recall all that I could of the attack.

"What team? What team was he wearing? On the baseball cap?"

"I think it was the A's," I said. "It was red cap."

"That's not the A's," Curtis Beaumont said. "The A's are green and yellow."

"You sure it had an A on it?" Hill asked.

"Yeah, it was turned around backwards," I said. "I saw it plain as day."

"The only team I know of with an A on a baseball cap is the Braves or the Diamond Backs," the lawyer said.

I didn't argue. I didn't care. I didn't see the significance.

Shay had two workable sketches of the three men that kidnapped Kyla Hudson. Honestly, I thought my work was done. What else was I to do?

"Now what?" I asked Louis Bennett.

"Now, you go for a ride with me, and Shay and Hill and we find the morons that decided to kidnap my god daughter." Bennett paused.

"Wait. What?"

"Cam, you are the only one who has seen the kidnappers. So, we need your eyes," Kyle Hudson said.

I looked from Bennett to Mister Hudson and back to Bennett.

"Think we know where to go. We just need you to ID the idiots that overstepped. That's it. We slap them around a bit for daring to snatch my god daughter and then we find Kyla, hopefully, before things get too out of hand," Bennett said, his hand on Mister Hudson's shoulder.

Chapter 7.

The Cadillac Escalade was a big SUV. The one that I climbed in with Louis Bennett was massive. There were three rows of seats and a cargo hold. With just four of us in the SUV the vehicle seemed cavernous.

We raced down the interstate headed south.

"Where are we going?"

"You know where everyone goes to hideout in this state," Bennett said from the passenger seat.

"The lawyer sent us the spaghetti list," the musclebound man sitting in the rear of the SUV said, looking at the notebook computer.

"Anyone we know?"

"Antonio Garibaldi," Hill said.

"Why do I know that name?"

"Ant is a low-level Guido with his hands in everything from gaming to real estate," Shay said from the front of the SUV. "Think he was somehow connected to a massage parlor we found one of the girls trying to hide in."

"Yeah, I remember," Bennett said. "Get in contact with Tip and see if he has tabs on either one of them," Bennett said.

"Also, according to Beaumont there are Wander Brett, David Charlotte, Brewer Collins and Cyril Paulson to consider," Hill said next to me.

"Okay, any of them have offices in Vegas?"

"Two," Hill said. "Wander Brett and Brewer Collins," said Hill looking at his phone.

"Get in contact with Tip and see if he knows either one of them," Bennett said. "Tell him that we are on our way and need a landing point." Bennett paused. "Contact both those offices and see if we can make an appointment to see either Wander or Brewer Collins."

"Antonio Garibaldi is working for Brewer Collins Group," Hill said. "Brewer Collins is a real estate group."

"Okay, set it up," Brewer said.

Hill nodded and texted Tip as the Escalade rolled toward the freeway.

The musclebound Hill dialed a number next to me and waited for someone to answer. I tried not to eavesdrop.

"Hello. My name is Michael Hillman. I am a representative of a very wealthy investor looking to talk with David Charlotte tonight about purchasing some property in or near the Las Vegas Strip. We would love to sit down and talk tonight if possible." Hill listened. "Great. Seven o'clock is fine. We'll meet you at your office at seven," Hill said on the phone. "Thank you."

There was a pause.

"Great," Hill said. "We do not have a big window of time."

He tapped his phone.

I nodded at Hill's subterfuge. We were headed to Sin City. I smiled at the irony of going to rescue Kyla from Sin City. It was my pastor that had preached and given me the idea of seeing this through no matter what the consequence. He had preached on love the day after my first date with Kyla and sealed my fate because of it.

The day after I went to the movies with Kyla Hudson, I awoke to the sound of gospel music. I opened my eyes in the early morning and made out my mother walking past my door headed toward the kitchen. A few minutes later she walked past again singing that catchy song going to her bedroom. I lay in bed listening to my mother singing some gospel song I had heard at least a dozen times before but couldn't place in my sleep filled head.

"Cam," my mother said with a voice trained for gospel from my bedroom door. "Get up baby. We have to be at the church at eight this morning."

I rolled over and looked at the clock. It was just turning seven o'clock in the morning. According to my calculations something was wrong. How did my mother need an hour to drive twenty minutes to our church?

"Cam? Get up," my mother said again from somewhere in the house.

I sat up. I opened my eyes and there on my wall opposite the foot of my bed sat a poster of Muhammad Ali. Muhammad Ali stared back at me as I blinked and tried to shake off the grip of sleep.

I sat in bed and in the murky morning light of my bedroom I took in the poster of Dorothy from the Wizard of Oz being frisked by a policeman, from Banksy. I looked to my bedroom closet and on that wall was the glossy picture of the movie poster V for Vendetta. It was the only movie poster in my room.

"Cam? Are you up?"

"Yes. I'm up," I said, climbing out of bed in my pajama shorts and T-shirt. I let my feet touch the hardwood floor and paused letting the wood and my feet reacquaint themselves before moving. I sat and blinked and blinked and sat for a full minute before climbing to my feet.

My mother walked past my bedroom door and smiled. She was wearing a green dress with gold highlights in it as she passed. Her hair was pinned up and in a tight bun of finger thick black braids.

"We have to leave no later than a quarter to eight," my mother said and disappeared.

I walked to the bathroom and tried to find my legs. I flipped on the bathroom light and walked past the bathroom mirror. At the end of the sink stood the toilet. On the other side of the toilet was a bathtub and shower. I blinked and looked at the shower curtain that I had picked out long ago. I smiled at the Spiderman shower curtain. I stood and prepared to relieve myself and tried not to miss the bowl.

"Cam," my mother said as I washed my hands, face and brushed my teeth. I put on my deodorant and slipped into a clean set of underwear. I grabbed a clean pair of jeans and slipped on a pair of socks and my Air Jordans. Dressed in a T-shirt, jeans and sneakers I leafed through the four dress shirts in my closet for something appropriate to wear to church.

"Hurry up and get dressed. Breakfast is ready," my mother called as I finally stepped into our kitchen dressed in a light blue collared shirt for a light breakfast before church. My mother was dressed and ready to leave by the time I arrived at the kitchen table.

She was straightening the kitchen and wiping the counter as I sat.

"How was the movie?"

"It was fine," I said with a grin.

"That's it? That's all I get?"

"Well, I told you we were going to the movies. So, I went to the movies. We went and watched something," I said picking at my eggs.

"What did you go and see?"

"Mom," I said, knowing that I could not remember the movie I sat in the night before.

"You don't remember?"

"I remember," I said, trying to sound convincing.

"You know I raised you? Right?" My mother asked, looking at me over her glasses. "You know I can tell when you are lying."

"I'm not lying," I said, again trying to sound convincing.

"Cam, we are about to go to the church house, and I cannot have God almighty strike you down before we get there because you are lying to me this morning," my mother said, looking at me seriously.

"Okay," I said, giving in. I shook my head. "I know it was the one with two guys fighting against each other about something."

"Cam, that's every movie ever made," my mother said with a laugh.

"Yeah," I said with a nod. "I was sort of distracted."

My mother looked at me seriously. She studied me like I was a bug under a microscope.

"No, I don't mean like that," I said. "It was just different." I paused. "I don't know. I think I like her."

"Don't get too far ahead of yourself," my mother said. She laughed that Sunday morning, but it wasn't a mean laugh. She smiled at me, like I was her baby again.

Every Sunday mom drove us in her BMW to church. She liked driving in the luxury of the BMW sedan. The BMW was her reward for hard work.

I didn't even ask to drive knowing her answer before I would ask. Instead, I simply climbed into the passenger seat and sat as my mother reversed her 520i out of the driveway and leisurely drove us through Highland Hills and to church.

Henderson Church of Christ was not a mega church. It had been a small factory at some point when Robert Westinghouse and his wife, Vivica, decided to buy the property and convert it to a church. The church had been transformed and under a year it was the new home of Foothill Church of Christ. There was room for one thousand people. The property had room enough to include a church office and five offices for the pastoral staff.

That Sunday, the day after the Kyla Hudson date, my mother and the small choir sang their three songs they practiced all week. The first song was a praise song led by Vickie Nicole Marsh. VNM thought she was the next big thing in gospel and her songs were heartfelt but loud and spirited at nine o'clock in the morning. VNM was dressed in a small white fez like pillbox hat, a choker of pearls around her thick neck and a powder blue dress that made her look a little like a tube of toothpaste.

After the praise song there was an opening prayer by one of the deacons that was supposed to be a welcome to the church.

After the opening prayer there was another gospel selection by Krystal Richardson. Now, unlike VNM, Krystal Richardson was this petite beauty with an intensity to her that made most uncomfortable to laugh or play around her. She was a mother of three and possessed a delicate voice. That Sunday Krystal Richardson was dressed in a light blue summer dress that was cut in the front to resemble an arrowhead and showed off her curvaceous shape. She too wore a strand of pearls around her neck.

She sang VaShawn Mitchell's "Nobody Greater" and after the song the church was amped up for the Word. Before the Word was delivered though, there was an offering. The three or four hundred attendees dug in their purses, pocketbooks and wallets and gave.

Then Pastor David Westinghouse stepped to the podium dressed in his blue robe with a red overlay and red cuffs. He was a round headed man with piercing eyes and a straight nose above an always serious smirk. Westinghouse was in his seventies, according to my mother, and the middle son of six siblings. The two elder Westinghouse's, Delilah and Frederick, lived out of state and had not been to Foothill since I was alive and attending church.

The pastor was the oldest of five. Two lived out of state. The other three of his siblings lived in Henderson. There was Donald, Sabrina and Tamika, the youngest. They all worked for the church.

On the pulpit with Pastor Westinghouse was his quiet and loving wife. His wife was dressed in a beautiful yellow and white dress that had a high collar and fell to her ankles. Her hair was brushed into a loose bun. In her ears sat two diamond studs. At seventy, Vivica Westinghouse was a sturdy and graceful woman, sitting on the dais along with the half dozen ministerial staff.

"Good morning, everyone," Pastor Westinghouse said with a cursory look to the congregation as he placed his Bible on

the podium and adjusted the microphone which hung from a microphone stand next to the podium.

He adjusted the microphone until it was just right. Then he opened the Bible and looked to the crowd that morning. Pastor Westinghouse smiled and flipped through his Bible for a particular page. He looked up from the Bible, distracted.

"Too often, when I walk up to this podium, I find myself unsure how I will be used. I come here with a plan. I pray. I study. I prepare and craft a message for the service. Yet, sometimes, for all my plans, prayers and study He steps in," Pastor Westinghouse said, pointing upward with his finger. He looked out over the congregation and paused. "He steps in and takes the thoughts and plans and prayers I have set for today and decides on a different course." Westinghouse paused again. He placed both hands on the podium and looked out into the quiet of the church. "Today, He has stepped in. Thank God. He has effectively taken over the message before I can say one word I wrote."

The pastor closed his eyes.

"Before I came out, I jotted down some notes He had given me. I pray the words I am about to say fall upon you like manna and feed you spiritually and emotionally. Pray with me, brothers and sisters, that this message touches those with hardened hearts and stiff necks that have no need for the same old same old. To those today, if you stay with me until the end, you will realize that this message is not new at all but couched in the truth of the gospel and the God we serve."

Pastor Westinghouse prayed out loud for the divine presence to fall upon him and remove his human frailty and to become a vessel for the divine.

There were always times at Henderson Church of Christ that Pastor Westinghouse's message seemed singularly directed to me, but it was a rare thing indeed when all the words touched me.

"Today, my brothers and sisters I do not helm this ship as I usually do. As I stand here, before you I am captain, the shepherd still, but the unseen, all knowing directs this message. So, bear with me."

Pastor Westinghouse was not a big man. He was not six feet tall. He, just sixty-eight inches tall. With a soccer ball-like head, a small chin, big hands, long legs and his serious attitude most never imagined Westinghouse to be a man of God. He appeared to be many things, but not a man of God.

"I like to present my case simply. I find a Bible verse or message or parable and then attempt to clumsily interpret it. But today, my plans were subverted by the will of our Lord Jesus Christ."

Westinghouse placed his big hands on either side of the pulpit and looked out over the gathered congregation. He breathed deeply.

"I say "subverted," but I mean overridden. Over written?" The pastor paused. "God's plans are not our plans. So, I surrender. I present myself a willing instrument for the Lord Jesus Christ." He paused.

"Let us begin. In the Bible Christian and non-Christian know the Bible verse I will reference, and many are familiar with it because it is seen often at sporting events, especially football. John 3:16. I have to believe most know this, but I begin there today. I will read for clarity.

"For God so loved the world that He gave His only begotten Son, that whoever believes in Him should not perish but have everlasting life."

"Too often, as Christians, we are told that God is love. Jesus told us to love our brothers as we love ourselves. So, to be Christians we are asked to venture out into the streets and highways with love in our hearts in spite of the dark and evil world that surrounds us. We are instructed in unsaid and said instructions to turn the other cheek in the face of a wrong. We are asked to love those that do not love us. We, as Christians, are told it is better to love than hate. But, today, here and now, I ask a simple question of all those that can hear my voice: 'What is this thing called love?'"

"For God so loved the world that He gave His only begotten Son."

"The Lord has been working on me all week in preparing me for this message and I was unaware," the pastor said, smiling to the congregation. "I have been attacked on all sides this week. I know that I am not unique in attacks. If I asked now, I know that many might shout and say, "Amen" at the continual assaults you and I have dealt with this week, if not even this morning before this service. It is to these attacks that I want to encourage all who find themselves under attack and for those who are about to be attacked, there is a lesson for you as well.

"The Bible talks of love often," Pastor Westinghouse said. "In my learning I was taught that the ancients, the Jews, the ones who cobbled together the Bible we have today, knew that the Greeks, who taught the others, used love not as one thing but four.

"For God so loved the world."

"There is familial love. That is the love that we know with a mother and child. That love is familial. Family love. Now, we know that familial love is based on a connection usually a bond between family members. It is an example of God's love on earth. God is a teacher. He is showing us daily what is possible here on earth.

"The next love is brotherly love. Philial love is another way to describe brotherly love. It is why Philadelphia is called the city of brotherly love. Now, brotherly love is not based on family, but friends. It is another example of love on earth. Jesus talks of this love. When he says love your neighbor, He is not referring to your closest familial relation, but a stranger, an outsider from your familial circle. In our neighborhoods, with so much change, single parent homes, we find many comfortable with the idea of brotherly love. It is not a replacement of familial love. It is not better or worse. It is simply another form of love God has ordained.

"Now, I know many of you are aware of the love that has been twisted and abused and turned inside out to sell bubblegum to soap to cars. That abused love is sexual love. As I stand here before you, I would be the biggest liar if I did not admit that sexual love is incredibly tempting. We are fleshly beings. We are made of flesh and blood. God has mandated that we be fruitful and multiply. We are hardwired to have sex. Yet, sex is not love. Love is not sex. Sexual love is a love of sex. Again, like the other two loves this is God ordained. God made us and knew we would have these feelings."

Pastor Westinghouse paused and sipped at a glass of water sitting on a shelf in the podium. He looked out and over the congregation.

"Usually, when I am preaching and pause and look up, there are some tired faces and souls that have had long nights and are resting their eyes,"

Pastor Westinghouse said. "Not today. We are talking about love, and everyone is listening."

"Finally, there is Godly love. I have read time and time again that Godly love is the spiritual love. That love is the love that we all aspire to display."

Westinghouse paused again. He gripped either side of the podium and took a deep breath.

"I said all that to get here," the pastor said. "I am about to be a little controversial. God is the father. God is the head of the body of the church. God is a protector. He is a defender. He is a destroyer. Yet, he is also love. We have been told time and time again that God is love. As the head of the church God can be an angry God. He has killed. He has blinded. He has smote more people than I can ever number. Yet, He is love. He is the definition *of love, but He is vengeful. As Christians we should be striving to be like God and Jesus if we are to be recognized as Christians."*

Pastor Westinghouse wiped his sweating brow.

"Yet, here is the lesson, the understanding, the revelation. I think that God created two forms of those four loves. There is the soft love and there is also the hard love," the pastor said, looking out onto the congregation.

Cameron, who had been sitting in the rear of the church, started paying attention to the sermon. He leaned against the pew and found himself listening.

"What is soft love?"

Pastor Westinghouse asked. He paused and looked out over the congregation. "I think that most are familiar with soft love. It is the love that most believe God has told us to display to others. Love one another. Love instead of hate. Love our neighbor," the pastor said, pausing to catch his breath.

"Now, as Christians, we are taught that love is kindness. We are to love despite. We are to love in the face of hate. In this dark and wicked world, we think that is counter to our survival. We are witnesses to the evil waiting for those that believe there is only one type of love. There is not only the soft love."

The pastor nodded and let his words sink in. He looked across the heads that nodded and agreed.

"We have been taught our love makes us soft,"

Pastor Westinghouse said. He stopped and looked from the front to the rear of the church. He took another deep breath.

"Yet, we know instinctually that there is another love. God does not only believe in soft love. He has another type of love. There is also hard love."

Pastor Westinghouse smirked. He leaned on the podium and looked out at the congregation like he was about to wow everyone. "God has this hard love that is so different than the soft love we default to when we think of love. He shows this other love in nature to make us aware of the other type of love. We see this hard love in the familial love. We learn that it is necessary to reject the love we receive as children. We cannot stay in the soft love as we grow. We must make hard decisions in love as we grow. We must separate. We must move away from the soft love and create a different type of love. We mature and our love matures as well. In that move we create a hard love."

Pastor Westinghouse was teaching. He was trying to emphasize a new point.

"We are not made to be doormats from our love. Jesus was no doormat. He was no milk toast, weak kneed ninny. Jesus, our example, as Christians, was no soft love scaredy cat. He was the son of God. He never wanted us to be walked upon. In Bethlehem, he loved and fought with that hard love. His hard love drove out demons. He professed His hard love. In that love there was nothing he was afraid of."

Pastor Westinghouse wiped his brow and looked down at his Bible. He smiled. He placed a hand on his Bible and looked back up.

"Some may recall the man that told us to love our brother was also the very same man that chased the criminals and opportunists from the temple twice. His love of those seeking God outweighed his philial love of the criminals impeding, blocking, the people seeking of the Lord." He paused.

"What type of love was that? Brothers and sisters that was the Godly hard love that has been twisted and flipped on its head to make us, as Christians, believe something else. We are not to tolerate anything in the name of love. I wish to point out that Jesus' love of children was the hard love that I am talking about. It is the example that we should aspire to and not the pie in the sky soft love that many suggest."

Pastor Westinghouse turned and looked to the ministry. The ministers and their wives were all bobbing their heads in agreement with the pastor.

"I will tell you. The brotherly hard love of Jesus was on full display when he looked at those doing wrong and corrected them. Remember Jesus loved everyone, but he used his hard love and a whip to run the money changers from the temple."

He raised his hands as many in the congregation seemed ready to revolt or praise.

"Now, I know some greater than me Christians will say that is not their Jesus. Their Jesus is all soft love. But Jesus did not tolerate hypocrisy. He did not swallow insults. He did not truck with liars. He overturned tables and chased grown men from a temple, twice. Jesus loved those that were unlovable. He dared a crowd that was hellbent to stone a woman who has been caught red-handed in the act of adultery. That was soft love. Jesus is loving. He wanted his father, our God, to be proud." The pastor paused. *"It is interesting that now, in our day and age, we have taken the hard love of Jesus who ran men out of the temple twice because they hampered the believers from getting close to God, to only be the turn the other cheek Jesus. This soul that stepped down from heaven clothed in flesh did not come to accept everyone. As love, His love was not for everyone."* Pastor Westinghouse smiled. He nodded.

"So, I say that if we are to be Christians then we should be like our Lord Jesus. Jesus who loved everyone. Jesus who exhibited hard love when his soft love could not convince those hard hearted."

People hummed and agreed. The message was beginning to resonate.

"The last point I wish to make is that if you have Godly love, it transcends the here and now. Yet, we are here now."

Pastor Westinghouse said with a wry smile.

"We are striving toward Godly love." He paused, thinking. *"I know there are some that will tell you they are already spiritual beings, but they are not being honest. We are all striving for that goal. Until we do, we must be aware that our love, soft or hard, is*

measured. It is one part familial, one part brotherly, one part sexual and one-part Godly love. To be honest, that last part is usually the smallest part. We all strive to be better, but do not fool yourselves into believing that you see people as trees. We are not there yet. None of us are. So, we are to love those we can. We are also to help those we can. Yet, when those that are unlovable, they, we must approach, with the hard love of God. Those that cannot be approached with the soft love of God must be convinced with hard love. Jesus did not cast out devils with soft love. He beat back the devil with a hard love. Disrupt the criminals that would rob, steal and kill you and yours. There is no greater love than for one to lay down his life for the life of his brother."

The pastor ended the service, and everyone climbed to their feet. I climbed to my feet and shook hands with the half dozen kids my age as he headed to the front of the church to meet my mother. Kids I had met and gotten to know said goodbye.

At the end of the service my mother said her goodbyes, and the two of us headed home.

Once on the still lightly traveled freeway the Escalade seemed to move on rails. The SUV being so big absorbed all imperfections of the road. The noise disappeared as Bennett turned on the car stereo and the gigantic space was filled with the sound of pop music.

For a few minutes the Escalade just moved along with the music. The traffic was light at that hour as Shay drove the SUV toward Sin City.

As we drove, I tried to remember the last time he had been in Las Vegas. I knew it was a weird idea since I lived in Henderson, but most people that lived in Nevada did not live in Las Vegas or not the Las Vegas with the Strip and the glitz. Most people lived on the outskirts of Las Vegas in North Las Vegas. I thought about Boulder City and Mesquite that bordered Las Vegas proper. I had been to all those other cities more than Las Vegas.

In the last year I had been to Las Vegas maybe less than a dozen times.

"So, tell me what you're thinking," Shay said.

"Well, this ain't rocket science," Bennett said. "Most crimes are committed by people that know the victim."

"You thinking this is someone who knows Kyla?" I asked.

"No, I'm not thinking that," Bennett said and laughed. "I am thinking that one of those realtors is probably involved."

Shay kept driving.

A few miles before the airport traffic started to build. The traffic and rush hour were negligible as the Escalade pushed into Las Vegas proper.

I looked off and into the desert horizon and watched as one plane landed and then another. The Las Vegas airport was always busy and not too far away.

We passed the Las Vegas sign which stuck out like an angry tongue to all that approached the main city center. It sat on the median where a couple of tourists were gathered to take the required photo to prove they had made it to Vegas.

"Roll down the Strip," Bennett said. "We got some time," the finder of lost things said. "Head to...Sahara Avenue. I think we got time to swing by and see David Charlotte."

Chapter 8.

Shay drove down the Las Vegas Strip and the Las Vegas sign shrank in the rearview as the Escalade moved toward and then past the iconic Excalibur and the Tropicana Casino and Hotel and Planet Hollywood and Bally's. Crossing Flamingo Avenue, I smiled at the old Flamingo Casino and Hotel and then Caesars and the LINQ and Harrah's. A few minutes later the sound of cannons and the smell of smoke in the air signaled Treasure Island's pirate show. The Venetian sat on the far end of the Strip, just a block away from the Wynn Casino and Hotel.

On the other side of Desert Inn Road was what most considered old Las Vegas, or at least, the beginning of old Las Vegas. Below Desert Inn Road was Circus Circus Casino and Hotel, the Marriott and the Sahara Casino and Hotel. All the multi-million-dollar hotels and casinos fell away once the Escalade crossed Desert Inn Road.

Shay slowed and turned left and pointed the Escalade toward the freeway. Louis Bennett looked back and into the rear of the SUV and Hill nodded.

Shay turned on her turn signal and cut across the three-lane intersection and turned into the parking lot of one of the buildings sitting near the freeway.

"Okay," Bennett said. "This shouldn't take too long. Just feeling out this guy. You can wait in the car Cam. Shay will make sure you're safe."

Shay parked.

Hill and Bennett climbed out of the SUV.

The pair walked to the entrance of the building and entered.

"How long you think this is going to take?"

"How long?" Shay asked from underneath the steering wheel. She looked back at me through the rearview mirror. "I don't know, kid. As long as it takes."

I frowned at Shay's response. I clenched my teeth and tried not to think about the driver's non-answer.

"I know you are going to ask me some more questions, but before you do," Shay said, looking back into the rear of the SUV and at me. "So, Cam, can I ask you a question?"

I smiled at the question. I nodded.

"How come you care so much about Kyla?"

I thought about what Shay was asking. I tried to piece together the right words. I wanted to say that my pastor had delivered a sermon and in it he had explained every type of love we experience. I knew that I cared about Kyla and that my hard like had changed into a strong feeling that was borderline scary. I didn't want to say that I loved Kyla too soon. I liked her. I had strong feelings for her. I figured if and when I said that I loved Kyla it should be Kyla he was the first to hear it not Shay.

"Well, I guess, that I invested a lot in Kyla, if that makes any sense," I said, clumsily. "I only really had a relationship with my friends, my mom and... I mean, that's it," I continued, thinking. "I really like Kyla. I don't think that it was right to have her snatched in front of my eyes."

"What you think? You going to save her?"

"No, I ain't her savior, but I want her to know that I didn't just check in and check out when things got tough," I said, finally.

Shay smiled at my words.

Before Shay could say or do anything Hill opened the Escalade's rear door and climbed in. I scooted over to give the musclebound man in a hoody room. Suddenly I was seated directly behind Shay.

"Where's Bennett?" Shay asked.

Louis Bennett opened the passenger side door of the Cadillac and climbed into the cab of the SUV. Bennett did not seem happy or upset or very emotional after his and Hill's visit to David Charlotte.

"Everything okay?" Shay asked.

I looked at the profile of Bennett and then Hill, who was already on his phone.

Bennett nodded.

"Everything is hunky dory," Bennett said, thoughtfully. "I think David Charlotte is a snake and someone I wouldn't trust further than I could throw him, but he doesn't seem the type to kidnap someone's kid."

"Why you say that?" Shay asked.

"I guess because he has kids, based on the pictures in his office," Bennett said. "No one is going to kidnap someone's kids if his own kids could be a target. That just seems logical."

"Besides, he is in this off the Strip building, which shouts low-rent and he's trying to present himself as a big time Las Vegas realtor when most of his listings are in Henderson," Hill said.

"Someone who is going to kidnap someone is going to be a little more desperate," Bennett said. "So, we have to look elsewhere."

"Are you sure?"

"Think so," Bennett said.

"Okay," Shay said. "Where to?"

Bennett looked back. Hill was looking at his phone. He looked up noticing the quiet in the Escalade.

"Tip said he was headed to the Stratosphere. He had a lead," Hill said, with a smile.

"Okay," Bennett said. "We're heading to the Stratosphere."

"Got it," Shay said, putting the Escalade into gear.

Hill looked down at his phone and pouted.

"What?"

"Antonio Garibaldi is out on the Strip somewhere," Hill said. "His office is trying to locate him and trying and set-up a meeting with you."

"Okay," Bennett said.

By the time Shay pulled onto Desert Inn Road again the sun had set and Las Vegas had begun its transition into Sin City. I sat in the seat behind Shay and looked out the window and across the street and traffic. Minutes before arriving at Sahara Avenue where David Charlotte rented an office there had been maybe a handful of people on the sidewalks. Now, as we drove toward the overpass there were dozens of people dressed in shorts, skirts and dresses and already drinking all manner of beverages.

Sahara Avenue once on the other side of the freeway and closer to the Las Vegas Strip divided the bigger and megalithic hotels and casinos of Las Vegas from the older, but not the oldest, Las Vegas iconic casinos and hotels, which included the Stratosphere.

Shay turned the Escalade left and back onto the Las Vegas Strip.

Just a short ride from Sahara Avenue sat the Stratosphere.

"How come you think they came here?" I said, finally to anyone who wanted to answer.

"Seriously?" Hill asked.

I nodded looking at the back of Bennett.

"Yeah," I said.

"Compared to everywhere else on the Strip this the quiet side of the Strip."

"Less lights," Hill said.

Yet, on the more deserted end of the Strip below Sahara Avenue there was not as much activity. There were people on the streets walking, but the numbers were dribs and drabs. It was nothing like the elbow-to-elbow crowd back on the other side of Desert Inn Road.

"Less everything," Hill said with a shake of his head. "If you want to see the wild side of Vegas head down to Old Las Vegas and Fremont Mall. That place can be a zoo."

Old Las Vegas, where the Fremont Mall sat in all its glory, was another mile and lifetime away. I had been to Old Las Vegas a few times, but it wasn't my favorite part of Vegas. I really didn't have a favorite part of Vegas. All I know is that I personally avoided going to that part of Las Vegas.

There were seedier hotels, motels and casinos down in the Old Las Vegas. It had good parts to it, I presumed, but it was not a place I chose to investigate. Although there were police down in Old Las Vegas there was still a lot of crime compared to the biggest money-making part of the Strip, which made sense.

If you were going to get robbed, it was more likely to happen in Old Las Vegas than on the Strip. There were robberies on the Strip, but those robberies were few and far between the criminal activity that took place between Sahara Avenue and Old Las Vegas.

Thankfully, I thought, we weren't heading to the true Old Las Vegas.

"It's also the part of the Strip that is less than a bill a night," Hill said.

"It is incredibly affordable," Shay said from the driver's seat.

"I think the main reason is that there aren't as many eyes as possible watching here," Bennett said.

Shay turned the Escalade into the circular driveway of the Stratosphere.

"Shay, pull down a little to make the valets pause," Bennett said, letting the Escalade roll a few more feet away from the entrance to the hotel before stopping.

I looked around and noticed there was security and cameras at the entrance to the hotel.

As soon as Shay hit her brakes two valets popped up from behind columns in the front of the Stratosphere and jogged to the Escalade. They both had big smiles plastered on their faces and were wearing black vests, bowties and black trousers. On their vests were nameplates.

Bennett and Hill climbed out of the Escalade.

"Give us a minute to find Tip," Bennett said at the door. "We should be back soon," he added closing the door and walking to the entrance of the hotel with Hill and disappearing inside.

"Who is Tip?"

"He's the people person of the group," Shay said from the driver's seat.

I scooted back over to my original seat so that I could see Shay's profile.

"What does that mean?"

"He has a certain way about himself. People like him. He has this personality that people like and they are usually willing to talk to him about just about anything," Shay said with a smirk.

I took in what Shay said. I thought about Bennett and his crew. There was Mister Louis Bennett, the finder of lost things, a hard-nosed, no-nonsense character. There was Hill, not sure if his name was really Michael Hillman, and someone willing to bend the truth to get a foot in a door, then there was Shay Taylor, the creative one-time basketball player. She was smart and intelligent and friendly. Now, I was supposed to meet the people person of the crew.

A few minutes later Bennett and Hill came out with this thin, six foot four, gangly kid dressed like a valet. The tall kid seemed odd as a valet in Las Vegas. He looked like he should have been playing basketball or changing the lights in streetlights or something that utilized his height better than climbing in and out of cars for the Stratosphere.

"So, like I said, your friend told me that you would pay me for this information," the valet said, looking around nervously.

"Why are we going to pay you?"

"Because I know something you don't," the tall valet said. "And if you want you can go and try and find this information that no one else has and make your trip an extended nightmare of dead ends."

Bennett stepped forward. Hill reached out and restrained Louis Bennett.

"You trying to scam me, Buddy?"

"No scam," the valet said. "Real truth."

I listened as the three talked at the fender of the Escalade.

"So, peep, peep," the valet said, standing on the sidewalk and looking up and down for anyone. "I was supposed to tell you that your friend Tip had to go to the MGM Grand, but he told me to be on the lookout for you and tell you to head to Circus Circus first. He left something for you in the casino. He left and headed to MGM Grand because it was an emergency."

"How do you know?" Hill asked, confused.

"Like I said earlier, I know Tip and I told him I would look out for you," the valet said.

"Okay, Buddy," Bennett said, annoyed already. "Say, I believe you. You delivering messages to me from Tip." Bennett looked at Hill and Hill looked at Buddy and shrugged. "Why wouldn't Tip contact me himself instead of tell some rando to give me information?"

"Because he gave me something when he came here earlier and asked if I knew what to do with that something. So, I told him that I might know someone. Now, I told him I would do this something for a price. He had to go to the MGM for a personal. I didn't really pay that much attention. He said that he would text you, so you knew I was legit. Like I said, he had some kind of emergency."

"What kind of emergency?"

"He didn't say," Buddy said. "He did say that you would pay me for the information."

"Pay you for what?"

"Okay," Buddy said, pointing to Bennett. "Good question. The way Tip told me is that this is a fluid situation. There are a few parts to it. So, he had to go to the MGM Grand to make sure that... one part didn't get away. I was supposed to help out. He left something with me and now it is at Circus Circus. Now you are supposed to pay me to get what you are supposed to get."

"How in the fuck is going to Circus Circus going to help us out?"

"Well, the way I hear it you are looking for someone and this something is supposed to help," Buddy said, his hands in his trouser pockets.

Bennett exhaled.

"The way I also hear it is the guys you are looking for are a part of this something," Buddy said.

"Are the people we're looking for at Circus Circus?"

"No, I don't think so. But that isn't something I was supposed to be working on. My job is to get something for Tip," Buddy said with a snicker.

"Does Tip know where the people are?"

"I don't know," Buddy said.

"How you not know?"

"I get paid to park cars and listen," Buddy said. "I get more money listening."

"You happen to listen good enough to know who these people are?"

"The free portion of this discussion is over," Buddy said, looking at Tip evenly. "I know that what I know is valuable. Tip said it was valuable and you would pay. So, I figure there needs to be a fair exchange for any more information," Buddy said. He added, "By the way, in Vegas, people are always looking for someone. Right? I figure it's worth..." Buddy pursed his lips like he was about to kiss someone.

"I say a bill for your time and inconvenience," Hill said with a smirk, holding a hundred-dollar bill in between his fingers.

"Man, you cheaping out on me? Tip said this information was important to getting that certain someone back?"

"Okay, two bills," Hill said pouting, suddenly holding two hundred-dollar bills between thumb and forefinger.

"Okay," Buddy said, taking the money from Hill. "Ask for Ronny. He's a tall, lanky brother. Works at the gift shop on the western entrance." Buddy smiled. "He was supposed to print something and make two copies of a video. Just tell him Buddy sent you."

"Okay, thanks," Hill said.

Bennett and Hill climbed back into the SUV. Shay and I waited for Bennett to speak.

Shay looked to Bennett. I looked to Hill and then to Bennett. Hill looked like he had been given an Algebra problem.

The Escalade just idled as Bennett sat in the passenger seat.

Shay looked at Bennett.

"Okay, so we're heading to Circus Circus," Bennett said. "Think that this might be a snark hunt. So, need to be on your toes, everyone."

"Should we walk?"

"We aren't tourists," Bennett said to Hill in the rear seat.

"But it ain't that far," Hill said, with a smile.

"Hud just texted," Bennett said. "They got a ransom note. They want a quarter of a mil," Bennett said, reflectively.

"That doesn't sound like a whole helluva lot of cash for someone like Hudson," Hill said.

"Think it's to annoy not bankrupt," Bennett said. Bennett added, "Hill, contact Tip and tell him to stay put at the MGM and we're headed to Circus Circus." Bennett pouted. "Tell him I don't like dealing with his people. Shay, drive," Bennett said.

The SUV was library silent. Hill looked down at his phone. Bennett sat in the passenger seat and sulked.

"Just got a text from Tip. He said to trust Buddy. He said he had a personal problem he had to deal with," Hill said.

A few minutes later, as the SUV moved slowly down Las Vegas Boulevard Bennett looked up from his phone and spoke.

"Watch everybody while we're here. Shay, you stay close. If we find my god daughter, we're jetting quick, fast and in a hurry," Bennett said.

The drive to Circus Circus was just about ten minutes. It didn't seem like anyone was in a talking mood all of a sudden. In the quiet of the ride from the Stratosphere to Circus Circus I found myself recalling my meeting with Kyla's father.

Having weathered the storm that was the Hudson dinner Kyla said that I was suddenly accepted by the man behind everything. It was a little odd. I didn't see what I had done to be accepted. I hadn't done anything to impress Mister Hudson.

"I think my dad was impressed that you weren't being all fake," Kyla said.

"Fake?"

"Yeah, he hates that," Kyla said. "He's told me time and time again to watch out for people interested in our money or fame."

I nodded. I thought about what Kyla was saying. I paused and looked at the delicious girl in front of me.

"You have a bunch of other boys come up to see your dad?"

"No," Kyla said, looking at me annoyed.

"So, how does he know I wasn't being fake?"

"Cam, stop it," Kyla said, with a slight pout.

"Okay," I said, reaching out and putting a hand on her shoulder.

"He liked you," Kyla said.

"What's not to like?"

Kyla laughed, then got serious.

"He had a lot of questions about you afterwards," she said, thoughtfully.

"Like what?"

"You know," Kyla said.

"I don't."

Kyla looked at me seriously.

"He wanted to know if we had," she paused looking at me and then looking away.

"Damn, really," I said, surprised how the conversation had turned. I suppose that it was a reasonable question. It had to come up. I was sort of glad he wasn't the type of guy that asked that kind of question over dinner, or after meeting someone.

"What did you tell him?"

Kyla shook her head at my question and smiled.

"What else did he ask?"

"I can't remember," Kyla said, a little embarrassed.

"He worried I'm trying to get you pregnant to take his money?"

"It's not like that," Kyla said.

"You think he's going to try and buy me off?"

"What?"

"Yeah, one of my friends said that rich people think that everyone has a price." I paused. We were sitting in the gymnasium after lunch and before the bell rang for classes to resume.

"You know that I'm not after your money, don't you?"

Kyla looked at me and smiled naughtily.

"You know I'm after that big brain of yours. It's the only way I'm going to get out of math this year," I said.

Kyla shook her head and we both laughed.

In the middle of the week Mister Hudson called me and asked me to come up to the house. I couldn't say no.

Afterschool I drove up to the gates of the desert palace. I noticed that there was a Maserati SUV and a Rolls Royce parked in the circular driveway. As I parked the Jetta behind one of the two Escalades, I could not help but think about the money spent to have all this security. It had to be a huge monthly bill. As I climbed out of the Jetta, I suddenly found myself thinking about what or who Mister Hudson was trying to protect himself from.

"Mister Weaver," Larissa said with a smile, dressed in her all-black outfit.

I studied the woman dressed in black and wondered idly if she was armed.

'Follow me, Mister Hudson is expecting you," Larissa said.

I followed.

"Hey, Larissa," I said, as we walked through the quiet interior of the palatial home. "What gives? Why is there all this security?"

"Well, there are a lot of people who don't like to see some rise up higher than they expect," Larissa said with her English accent.

"So, you are here to make sure that no one steals their stuff?"

"That and more," Larissa said.

That and more?

"Are you guys always armed?"

Larissa smiled.

I studied Larissa and though she didn't answer I knew her answer.

Larissa walked me to the exercise room. In the exercise room was all manner of weights and machines. It looked like a high school weight room but cleaner and with newer equipment. A black, baldheaded man with a great physique, who was wearing a Nike tracksuit, was monitoring Mister Hudson's activities when I arrived.

The man had a clipboard and a stopwatch. He looked up at Larissa and then me. There was a silent exchange between the two and I watched as he reached out and tapped Kyle Hudson on the shoulder to get his attention.

Hudson, short and stocky, was doing barbell curls. He looked to the baldheaded man and then to Larissa and then me. He did not smile seeing either of us.

"Cam," Kyle Hudson said with a determined look, dressed in T-shirt and sweatpants. He was working the barbells near a weight machine. "Give me a minute. I'm just finishing my workout."

I nodded and looked for a place to sit. I noticed that there was another man in the exercise room. He was oddly big. His arms and legs seemed inhumanly large.

The second stranger looked like one of those professional football players. He was easily six foot five inches tall and two hundred and fifty pounds of Grade A beef. He was wearing hooded sweatshirt and gray sweatpants. On his feet were new Nike Jordan basketball sneakers.

Larissa stood beside me.

I looked to the big guy stalking the equipment.

"Is that somebody?"

"Of course," Larissa said with a slight smile. She added: "Everyone is somebody."

"Naw, I mean, is he famous?"

Larissa smiled but did not answer.

No answer was an answer.

I sat and watched as Mister Hudson finished his workout.

"That's it for me today," Hudson said, and the trainer smiled and nodded.

With the words the man with the clipboard smiled.

"Good work today," the man said.

The giant dressed in sweatpants and sneakers toweled closed the distance between him and the realtor. The closer the giant came to the realtor the more I felt I knew him. I looked at him and his big muscles and gigantic body and I knew the giant was someone I had seen, but I could not recall where.

"You out?"

"Yeah," the giant said. "Remember what I need?"

"I got you," Hudson said with a thin grin. The two clapped hands. Hudson was easily a foot shorter than the gigantic man with biceps the size of my thighs.

The giant grabbed his tote bag and exited with the trainer, led by Larissa.

Alone in the exercise room Mister Hudson sat and stared at me. He did not move. So, I climbed to my feet, unsure why the powerful realtor needed to see me. I walked closer and sat on a bench near Kyla's father. Kyle Hudson smiled.

"Cam," Hudson said looking at me with an odd grin. "How was school today?"

"Good, sir," I said, watching him towel off.

"Well, I wanted you to come by before Kyla shows up to discuss a few things," Hudson said.

Two weeks after the dinner and Hudson was going to give me the heave-ho, I figured. Wes had said that the Hudson's were different kind of people and did not want people to threaten their empire. So, according to Wes, they might try to buy me off. Money was the commerce of their world, and any problem was answered using it. It only made sense that if I was a problem, they would use money to solve it.

"Sit down," Kyle Hudson said.

I sat on a bench and slipped off my backpack, realizing for some reason, I had brought it in from the car. Putting my backpack near my feet I looked at the father of the Hudson family and waited for him to speak.

"You want something to drink?"

I shook my head. I figured Mister Hudson was feeling me out before attacking.

"Okay, I'll cut to the chase. It was nice to meet you for dinner," Mister Hudson said.

I listened.

"It was nice to hear you explain your intentions with my daughter," Hudson said with a grin.

I didn't say anything. He hadn't asked a question.

"I have to admit that you are not what or who I expected Kyla to bring home to meet us," Kyla's father said.

I didn't react. I knew he had insulted me, but I let it slide. My mom had told me that sometimes it was better to kill the asshats with kindness. They always thought themselves better but when I sat there and did not react, I could see Mister Hudson react.

He smiled awkwardly.

"You're a nice kid, Cam," Kyle Hudson said. "My Kyla likes you and that says a lot."

I nodded, not knowing when her father was going to tell me the reason, he had invited me to his home. I watched her father sipping at his water bottle. He looked at me through his piercing eyes.

"So, I was curious if you could tell me what are your plans for the future? You know, the next five years? I'm curious. I mean, what are your plans?"

Finally, after what seemed like twenty minutes Mister Hudson asked a question.

"Well, sir, after I graduate from high school, I plan on going to college," I said, thinking of the colleges I wanted to go to that month. "I think that if I can, I want to do something with sports management. I'm not sure what is the best school for that, but I think I want to be a sports agent or a team manager. I like that," I said. I had more to say but chose to stop there.

Kyle Hudson studied me evenly. He just stared with that intense look that seemed part annoyance and part constipation.

"What do you do for fun, Cam?"

I smiled and stalled, thinking. Fun?

"Well, I like video games, a little. I play basketball, a little bit. Again, mostly for fun. Not too serious about sports. I like to go to movies." I paused, thinking. I tried to answer Mister Hudson honestly. "I don't know, sir. I swim. I go into Vegas, occasionally, and run through the casinos and arcades. You know? I'm still underage. That's it, I think sir."

"Video games? Basketball? Movies," Mister Hudson said, slowly. "Are you on the basketball or swim team?"

"No sir," I said. "I just like playing basketball and swimming and enjoying the water."

"What do you do in the casinos?"

"I'm still underage, sir," I said, with a grin. "I just like to go to the arcades and watch the security guards watch me and my friends as we walk through the casino and go and play video games." I added, "It's nice to get out of the house and do something a little different."

"Yes, I understand that, when we were kids, we did the same," Mister Hudson said.

"Yes, sir," I said, with a small smile.

"You ever been in trouble with the law?"

"No, sir," I said immediately.

Kyle Hudson nodded, silently. He had his workout towel in his hands and unconsciously was wringing it tighter and tighter in his hands.

"You do any drugs, Cam?"

"No, sir," I said, a little surprised at the question.

Mister Hudson looked at me evenly and held the look for a long time.

"Are you religious, Cam?"

"I am. I go to church every Sunday."

"Where?"

"We go to Highland Christian," I said. I smiled and added, "Do you know Pastor Westinghouse?"

"I do," Mister Hudson said, with a chuckle.

I nodded.

"How long have you been going there?"

"I don't know, sir," I said. "All my life. I don't think I've been at another church, ever."

"Pastor Westinghouse," Mister Hudson smiled. "I helped him get his building."

I listened. It seemed like I was supposed to say something, but I didn't know what to say. "Good" or "That's great" just didn't seem appropriate. I wracked my mind for the right thing to say but by the time I figured I could have nodded, and smiled Mister Hudson had moved on.

"What are your parents like?"

I didn't answer immediately. I didn't have parents. I had my mother.

"It's just me and my mom, sir," I said as evenly as possible.

"That's right," Mister Hudson said, bobbing his head.

"What's your mother do, for a living?"

"She works at the Mirage. She's in customer service. I think she's a manager."

Mister Hudson looked at me evenly.

"Right," he said.

"You keep in contact with your father?"

"No, sir," I said, looking at Kyla's father trying to determine if he was trying to make me angry.

"Why not?"

"I don't know why not, sir," I said, slowly. "My mom and dad split up long before I was really old enough to know him. He isn't in our lives." I paused, thinking. "Can't make something happen that is not there." I hesitated and added, "You can't make someone love you if they don't want to love you. My mom told me that."

Mister Hudson nodded. He looked as if he was preparing to say something important. He had a real pensive look on his face. "Are you looking for something Cam?"

I did not answer Mister Hudson then and there. I had to think about what he was saying. His words were very measured. It seemed like he had been waiting to ask that question and all the other questions were just a prelude.

"No, sir," I said, suddenly confused.

"Are you sure?"

"Yes, sir."

"Cam, everyone is looking for something," Hudson said.

"Well, that might be most people," I said, with a chuckle. "I'm not most people. The only thing I want right now is to be with your daughter for as long as she will have me." I paused. "I got one more year of Foothill and then hopefully college and sports management."

We sat around the mansion for about an hour and Mister Hudson walked me to his office on the second floor of his home. The office was one of the three bedrooms in between his master bedroom and Kyla's. In the converted bedroom sat a large kidney bean fingerprint etched glass table with two rows of drawers as legs holding the thick surface atop it. On the desk sat a monitor and an in and out box and stacks of papers. On one wall was a whiteboard that looked like it came from school. On the whiteboard was a calendar template and in each box several names, numbers and numbers. Beneath the whiteboard in one of those lighted cabinets were visible dozens of awards. On top of the cabinet were three large trophies.

On the opposite wall was a framed map of Clark County. Underneath the map sat two of those white vertical file cabinets.

The office was very cold and stark. On the top of the file cabinets were two awards.

"Cam, you know what a hypothetical is?"

I nodded as I stood in Mister Hudson's office.

He walked to a closet and stepped in briefly.

"Give me a second," Mister Hudson said entering the closet and a few moments later stepping out.

When he reappeared, I looked Kyla's father over for any weapon. I had watched enough movies to know any time someone disappeared and reappeared trouble was going to follow. I was looking for Mister Hudson to have a knife or a gun in his hand to end me.

As he looked at me, in my head, I was retracing my steps to the front door. I only had to get the attention of the security to stop any madness that might happen now, I thought.

"Okay, say, hypothetically, if I gave you ten grand to stay away from Kyla, hypothetically," Mister Hudson said, with a slight grin. "Would you accept it?"

I looked at Kyla's father and thought I had missed my opportunity to record him trying to bribe me. My phone was in my jean pocket, and I thought if I could casually fish it out and record him saying those exact words again. That was not possible.

"Well, Mister Hudson, I have to admit that there is no amount of money that would buy me off, hypothetically," I said. "I mean, I like your daughter. She's amazing. You know. She's your daughter." I paused, looking at Kyla's father suddenly saddened for the man that put so much stock in the power of money. "I mean, if you were in my shoes and you got a chance to be with Kyla would you care about anything else but being with her?"

Hudson stood there looking at me and then and there I figured that he either had a stack of cash behind his back or a .45ACP pistol. I was hoping that he had the cash rather than the pistol. He could put the cash down on his desktop and I wouldn't look at him sideways. If he had put a pistol down on the table, I would have to look at him differently.

"Mister Hudson, thanks for inviting me up to see you and for the conversation, but I think I'm going to go now," I said, backing out of the office and into the hallway and catwalk that led

back to the main portion of the mansion and the security members.

I walked to the stairs and was at the foot of the stairs when Mister Hudson appeared at the head of the stairs. I looked back as the security members looked past me and toward him.

Larissa appeared and of all the security members she was the only one I knew or had a working relationship with. Upon seeing her I instantly wondered why she was there and not at the high school.

Larissa watched as I pushed past the assembled and exited the house. I toyed with telling Wes and Lyle what Kyla's father had offered me, hypothetically. I climbed into my car and started the engine thinking if I should tell Kyla what her father had attempted to do. As I drove away from the Hudson mansion, I decided that I wouldn't tell anyone what Mister Hudson had said or done. It was between him and me. I figured that he was ready to use whatever I said against me. As I drove home, I wondered if Mister Hudson had taken me to his office to record my response. Luckily, I cared about Kyla and wasn't chasing her family's money.

I blinked and realized that I needed to talk to someone I could trust. I wanted to talk to my mom suddenly. I felt out of control. I looked to Shay and Bennett, and she smiled.

"You're sure you're, okay?" Hill asked, concerned.

"I want to call my mom," I said, feeling a little tightness in my chest with the words.

Bennett hearing me turned around in the passenger seat and looked at me with his gentle eyes.

"Call her," Bennett said. "We aren't kidnapping you. You are just here to identify one or two of the kidnappers. Once that happens you can go back to Henderson."

I nodded. I fished out my cell phone and dialed my mom while in the rear of the Escalade.

Shay stopped the SUV in the driveway about one hundred feet from the entrance. She sat and Bennett and Hill sat silent as church mice as I called my mother. The three adults didn't seem to pay attention to the call. They sat and looked at each other and had silent conversations with each other while I talked to my mother.

It was good to hear my mother's voice. She told me she had been called by Missus Hudson earlier. She told me before I could tell her anything significant that I should help wherever possible to get Kyla back. I agreed and hung up.

"Everything okay?"

I nodded.

"See? We're legit. We need you to ID these perps and then we get you back to Henderson. Easy peasy," Bennett said.

"Lemon squeezy," said Hill, with a big smile.

Shay drove into the hotel driveway and like the Stratosphere she pulled to the curb a few feet from the entrance. Bennett and Hill again climbed out of the Escalade.

"Cam, you stay here," Bennett said. "We just trying to put hands on this kid in the gift shop," he said and closed the Escalade door.

The two walked to the western entrance. The pair entered the entrance of the Circus Circus and disappeared.

Shay sat under the wheel of the Escalade and played on her phone while she waited. The long-limbed woman did not feel the need to talk. After a few minutes of silence Shay looked back into the rear of the Escalade and looked at me curiously.

"You, okay?"

I nodded. I tried to think if I should ask the million questions in my head. I looked at the tall and attractive woman behind the steering wheel. I took a deep breath.

"How is Mister Bennett going to find Kyla?"

Shay looked back and studied me. She smiled, just a little, before answering.

"I'm not one hundred percent sure," Shay said. "He has his ways."

"Does he do this kind of stuff often?"

Shay looked at me in the rearview mirror, smiling.

"More often than you would expect," Shay said. She smiled. "Why you asking?" Shay asked.

I smiled. I was curious. I had always been the curious type. I didn't tell Shay that. Instead, I said something about trying to understand how Bennett and Kyla's father were connected. Shay seemed to read my mind.

"We all went to UNLV at some point. I think Bennett and Hudson were friends before college or they met while in college," Shay said, looking at me with a grin.

"How long you been working with him?"

"For the last four years," Shay said with an easy smile.

"Did you play basketball at UNLV?"

Shay turned in her seat and looked me up and down. She was bigger than I imagined up close and personal. She had all the normal features of a woman, but everything seemed a little bigger, longer and more distinct.

"I did, but I got injured," Shay said, batting her long eyelashes.

"Was it your knees?"

"It is always the knees when you play ball," Shay said, with a glossy smirk.

"Do you live in Vegas?"

"Nope," Shay said. She smiled, thinking. "Does anyone really live in Vegas?"

"I suppose not," I said with a nod. I looked at Shay, curiously. "Are you and Mister Bennett in a... relationship?"

"Cam, I thought you were in a relationship with Kyla?" Shay asked, with a smile.

"I am."

"Then why you want to know my relationship status?" She asked.

I fell silent. I looked at my knees and thought how I got to this point. I looked back up and saw her smiling in the rearview mirror.

"How long you been with Kyla?"

"Nearly a month," I said, proudly.

"You the real deal?"

"I think I am as real as I can be," I said.

Shay did not speak for a moment. "You have to be the real deal," Shay said, more to herself than to me. "I think that this would be a little too much for most just trying to get close to someone. Most would fold under pressure," Shay said.

I didn't respond.

"I guess you either make a diamond or break something into glass under pressure," Shay said.

Again, I didn't say anything.

Shay looked at me in the rearview mirror and I held her gaze for a minute. She smiled. I smiled as a result.

"What do you do? I mean, you are crazy talented with that notebook," I said.

Shay shook her head. She shrugged, confused.

"For work? I do this and that. Today, I'm the driver. Tomorrow, don't know." She shrugged her shoulders. "I like being free to do what I want. I like being creative," Shay said.

"Creative?"

"Yeah. That's my thing," Shay said. "When I was at UNLV and basketball ended, I got into art and computers."

"Everyone have talents?" I asked. "You know? Among you?"

"Yeah. Bennett is the finder of lost things. That's his thing. Hill is our litigator. He knows all the laws and how to break 'em. Me, I am the creative." She paused. "Tip? He has people skills."

"But what do you guys do? Are you detectives? Bodyguards? Or something like that?"

"No, kid, we aren't anything like that. We just help people who need a little help, as simple as that."

"How come I never heard of you?"

Shay laughed. "How old are you? Thirteen?"

"I'm seventeen," I said proudly.

"We ain't aimed at bubblegum crew," Shay said, with a smile.

I laughed at Shay's insult. I hadn't chewed bubblegum in months.

"You guys good at what you do?"

"Yeah, we are good at what we do," Shay said with a smile.

"Can Mister Bennett find anything?"

"Damn near," Shay said. "Bennett has a certain set of skills. Those skills give him an incredible advantage when trying to locate lost things," Shay said. "It helps that Kyla is his god daughter," she added.

I paused after Shay said that. I had to think about what that meant. Before I could formulate my question Shay seemed to read my mind.

"Bennett is a bulldog. He is incredible at what he does. If anyone can find Kyla it's him," she said.

Chapter 9.

At the mention of Bennett, the SUV's doors opened. Bennett and Hill climbed in. Bennett sat in the passenger seat next to Shay. Hill sat next to me. The two recently returned sat in the spacious interior quiet. Bennett sat still in front of me and did not seem happy. Hill looked at Bennett and then back at me. I noticed that Hill had one of those manilla envelopes that people used for big documents on his lap. It was upside down and the metal clip to fasten the lip of the envelope. There was no identification on the envelope.

Hill was pouting. He seemed preoccupied. He also seemed upset about something.

"You get what you wanted?" Shay asked, turning to Bennett.

Bennett did not reply immediately. He seemed to be thinking. I looked from seat back that held Bennett to Hill. The muscular man seemed pensive as well.

"What did you get?"

Bennett lifted a manilla envelope just like Hill's and showed it to Shay. I craned my neck to see the envelope that Bennett was holding. I saw that the file folder was labeled: PRINT COPIES.

"Tip's source was just a guy he had given a copy of the video to from the mall," Bennett said. "He had the guy go through the video and print out all the visible faces between three thirty and five today," Bennett said, reflectively. "The video caught Cam and Kyla getting robbed and her getting snatched." Bennett let Shay look at the dozen or so of grainy printed pictures. I leaned forward and looked at the grainy shot of the white boy with the gun, the U-shaped puncher and the hooded third tough.

Shay took the folder and Bennett scratched his chin. He fell silent.

"The thing is that what Cam said was right. There were three guys that jumped them. But there was also one man, in the shadows, that seemed to be overseeing everything that looked awfully familiar to me for some reason," Hill said, continuing from the rear of the Escalade. He had a folder like Bennett's. I hoped that Hill had the same grainy photos as Bennett. "I think I know him. He's a d-boy from somewhere, that I think I know. Maybe he's from Old Las Vegas," he said. "I just can't place him."

Bennett adjusted in his seat and seemed agitated. He leaned back into the rear of the SUV. He looked at me with those dark and serious eyes.

"Cam, you said there were just three people that jumped you," Bennett said.

I nodded.

"But there were four people, according to the video," Bennett said, studying me like I was about to steal something.

"I only saw three," I said. I tried to replay the attack. Kyla and I had exited the mall. I was carrying Kyla's bags and the two Build-A-Bears we had made when the first guy with the crooked nose stepped in front of Kyla with a gun. I stepped forward. Then the second guy came out of nowhere and punched me. He hit me hard and all the bags I was holding went spilling onto the parking lot floor. The last person I remember was the oversized watch and medallion with a pistol on it. There was no one else.

Bennett sat in the passenger seat, thinking. Hill looked out the window of the rear of the Escalade. Shay sat under the steering wheel waiting. I didn't know what to do, so I just sat watching Hill silently.

"Now, my question is: What do realtors, kidnappers and d-boys got in common?" Bennett asked.

"Location. Location. Location," I said in answer to Bennett's question.

Bennett looked back and into the rear of the Escalade with a slight smile.

Shay looked at me in the rearview mirror and nodded.

"Let's head to MGM Grand and talk to Tip," Bennett said.

Shay put the Escalade into gear and pulled away from the hotel.

The Escalade rolled away from Circus Circus and back onto Las Vegas Boulevard.

"Where's Tip?"

Bennett and Hill stayed quiet. I looked at Hill, who seemed irritated. Hill was looking out the car window and seemed to be lost in thought.

"He just texted and said he was going to meet us at the MGM," Hill said, finally.

"Roger that," Bennett said.

The drive down Las Vegas Boulevard from Circus Circus was a strange ride. The family-oriented circus inspired casino and hotel sat on the other side of Desert Inn Road and as a result was considered the older side of the Strip. Everything south of Desert Inn Road was deemed the newer and higher end of the Strip. This was not necessarily so. The Mirage was below Desert Inn Road and so were half a dozen other glitzy hotels and casinos, but most elite resorts and hotels and casinos with residencies were found south of Desert Inn Road.

So, the drive from Circus Circus was like going from a two-candle room into a fully lit and vibrant theater with singers and dancers everywhere. back to MGM Grand took about twenty minutes.

The MGM Grand sat on the southern part of Las Vegas Boulevard. Everyone that went to the casino or the hotel were greeted by the golden lion in the entrance. Shay wheeled the Escalade into the circular driveway and found herself braking behind a Ferrari, a Humvee, a Corvette and a limousine.

"Tip just texted," Hill said. "He said meet him in front of the David Copperfield theater."

Bennett looked back at Hill and did not look happy. He turned back and was quiet for a moment. Shay pulled the Escalade up the driveway and slowed near the entrance.

"Okay, Shay, stay with the kid. Keep the car close. I'm not sure if this is our destination, all of a sudden," Bennett said as Shay pulled into the circular driveway of the MGM Grand and a handful of valets scrambled to open doors and help Bennett and the musclebound man out of the Escalade.

Shay smiled, having locked her driver's side door and rolled down the window to let the hot of the desert flash heat into the interior of the Escalade. The valet attempted to open the driver side of the Escalade. His bright smile melted when he was unable to open the door.

"Dropping off and waiting," Shay said to the valet who listened and instantly seemed disappointed.

"Please move up out of the loading and unloading zone," the valet said. The valet pointed up ahead.

Shay moved the Escalade up a little away from the loading and unloading zone. She parked. She rolled down the windows and turned off the Escalade.

"Hey," I said, with a smile. "Can I ask you another question?"

"Sure," Shay said.

"This kind of stuff happen a lot?"

"It happens," Shay said. "I wouldn't say a lot."

I nodded, thinking of how to ask the next logical question.

"What do you think is going to happen?"

"I ain't a fortune teller, kid," Shay said with a laugh. "The way I see it, we're chasing down a lead. We find the right lead and bingo, bango, bongo we find your girlfriend and you go home and have a quiet Thursday night or Friday morning."

"It's Thursday," I said, realizing that the day had morphed into this crazy Las Vegas adventure with me tagging along to ID kidnappers.

"Why didn't Mister Hudson want to call the police?"
Shay smiled but did not answer.
"I think he was pretty clear," Shay said.
"Why?"
"We can't trust everyone. It's as simple as that," Shay said.

"But I get the whole not trusting them, in general, but what happens when things get out of hand?"

Shay did not respond immediately. She pouted and then twisted her lips on her brown face. She turned around to look at me. Shay looked serious, suddenly.

"You know a long time ago there were these things called: "neighborhoods." In those neighborhoods we had people that looked out for each other. No one in those neighborhoods called the police for too much. In those neighborhoods, we had our own police, sort of. If there was a problem, there was always someone ready to jump in and fix it. We cared for each other. We looked out for each other," Shay said. She smiled from the driver's seat. "I think Bennett is a throwback to those times when we cared for each other and relied on each other."

"I know what a neighborhood is," I said, with a smirk.
"Do you?"
I nodded.

"Those neighborhoods were filled with people that cared about each other. They protected each other. You could go and stay over your neighbor's house while your parents were gone. It was an extended... family," Shay said.

I took in what Shay said. I didn't answer her. The neighborhood that she talked about was nothing like the neighborhood I lived in. It wasn't like the neighborhood Kyla lived in. Most of the people living in Henderson didn't know each other. In the nine or ten years I lived with my mom I could not recall a time that any of the neighbors inviting me to their homes.

"I get it," I said.

Shay nodded.

"Why do you think they took Kyla?" I asked Shay.

"I don't know, kid," Shay said. "I think everything here revolves around money. Hudson has a lot of money. So, the way I see it this is mostly about money or intimidation about money. You know? It's stupid territorial stuff."

"What do you mean?"

"Well," Shay said turning in her seat to look at me directly. "This world is a bunch of pieces of pie. There's all these people trying to be something and scratching and clawing to be something. I don't know," Shay said. "Maybe they think they are chasing the same money or... the money is limited?"

"What do you mean?"

Shay shook her head, thinking.

"How are they chasing the same money?"

"I mean they act like there are only so many apples or pies or... something and they aren't willing to lose that sale," Shay said. "So, they are trying to get an advantage, anyway they can."

"An advantage?"

"Yeah, leverage," Shay said.

"What? You think this is all about money?"

"Dollars to donuts it is," Shay said with a smile.

"What? You think it's like Mister Bennett said that this is someone the Hudson's know?"

"I wouldn't be surprised," Shay said with a smirk.

"Really?"

"Yeah," Shay said, nodding. "Most people, in our experiences, are robbed, killed, beaten or kidnapped by someone they know or someone they know planned it out in some way."

"For real?"

Shay nodded.

I was about to ask another question when Bennett, Hill and a stranger arrived at the SUV.

"This is Tip," Bennett said.

Tip climbed into the rear of the Escalade, and I scooted over and found myself sandwiched between Tip and Hill.

Tip was ruggedly handsome. He had the classic square features of a superhero. Tip was a dark-skinned man wearing what looked like a dark blue silk shirt open to show off his chest, a blue and gold robe rested on his small shoulders and blue silk pajama bottoms covered his legs. On his feet were butter soft Italian leather shoes.

On his head sat a beige Kangol. He had an athletic build. Around his neck was a finger thick gold chain with a thick gold Versace medallion hanging from it. On his wrist was a gold Versace bracelet. On his pinkie finger was a gold Versace ring.

"Shay, it's good to see you again."

"Tip, I see you every day," Shay said with a shake of her head.

"It's still nice to see you," Tip said with a perfect smile.

"You Cam? Heard about you. Sorry about how things went. Teach you to stay in school, I suppose," Tip said in a single breath. He smiled and turned his attention to Bennett. "So, I have a lead on the kidnappers," Tip said.

"Where?"

"The Venetian," Tip said.

Bennett sat in the front passenger seat and smiled.

I watched Bennett. He was the leader. Hill and Tip and Shay were characters, but Bennett was the main character.

"Where to boss?"

"The Venetian," Tip said from the backseat.

Shay did not pay Tip any attention. Shay looked at Bennett and smiled. Bennett was thinking.

Shay looked to Bennett. He gestured and she started the SUV.

"We'll head to the Venetian, first and see where Tip's lead takes us," Bennett said. "Hill? Did you ever get in contact with Antonio Garibaldi?"

Hill looked at his phone and shook his head.

The drive from MGM Grand to the Venetian wasn't very far. Sitting next to Tip I couldn't shake the idea of the coolest person in Las Vegas sitting next to me. He was sweetly perfumed, immaculately coiffed, flashy and incredibly confident.

Shay pulled into the driveway of the Venetian and as always was the case the valets buzzed about the Escalade.

Bennett and Tip stepped out of the Escalade and spoke to the valet.

The valet seemed a little surprised. He nodded. The valet pointed back behind the Escalade.

"Shay get the Escalade washed, by the time you get back, we should be ready to go," Bennett said to Shay.

He turned his attention to Hill and me.

"You two come with me," Bennett said and turned and walked to the front of the MGM Grand.

Everyone exited the Escalade as Shay drove away.

Near the front of the hotel Bennett paused.

"Tip? You see him?"

"Yeah, there he is," Tip said looking in the direction of three valets dressed in red jackets, white collared shirts, black bow ties and black trousers.

The shorter and slightly jumpy valet that Tip and Bennett cornered at the Venetian was a good-looking man in his late twenties with a pencil thin mustache and slightly crooked smile. He was well groomed and had a golden nameplate over his heart that read: Spank.

After the small talk ended Bennett stepped forward, a little menacingly, and studied Spank.

"Tell me what I want to know," Tip said.

"Well, I hear lots from here," Spank said. He looked left and right. "I get to hear things that most people say and don't think people hear and that information can be valuable."

Bennett looked at Spank and then back to Tip.

"I don't buy anything unless I inspect it, first," Bennett said.

"Well, I understand inspection of things. I work in credibility. So, I'll give you a freebie. If that information I give you is credible then you will have to pay me for the good information."

"Okay," Tip said.

"What do you know?"

"Okay, I know that you came from Henderson. You got that look that you lost something or someone. I suppose you need some help in finding that something or someone," Spank said.

Tip looked to Bennett.

Bennett nodded.

"Well, what was that worth?"

Bennett smiled.

Spank looked back past Tip and Bennett. The valets were helping men and women in and out of their cars.

"We'll make it worth your time," Tip said.

"I make about five hundred a night," Spank said.

Bennett dug in his pocket and pulled out a knot of cash. Spank watched as Bennett peeled off four bills. He handed the money to Tip.

"Let me make this simple," Tip said. "If what you tell me leads to something substantial, I'll sweeten the deal." He handed Spank some of the money.

Spank leafed through the bills and then looked at Bennett then Tip.

"Okay, the way I hear it a couple of LV wannabes were doing someone a solid. They were asked to follow some princess and report. If they had a chance to scoop her up, they were supposed to take her." Spank paused and looked at me. "The two wannabes snatched the princess at some mall. They decided to hide in plain sight. They arrived here and got spooked."

"Are they still here?"

"They got spooked and left a few hours ago. They are supposed to be at one of the fancier hotels and casinos or one of the hotels just off the strip. They came here first." Spank paused. "I can't guarantee where they are. If any valet I know sees them they'll get back to me."

"What are you the king of valets?" Hill asked.

"Yeah," Spank said with a crooked smile. "Something like that."

"Did they hurt her?" Hill asked.

"When I asked about the princess, they never said she was hurt," Spank said.

"Know anything about who was with them?"

"Well, I'm not too sure. All I know is that it was a couple of wannabes and the girl."

"Did they seem... strange?"

"How do you mean?"

"Like tweakers," Bennett said.

"Tweakers? No one said anything about them being drunk or high. That's the usual complaint," Spank said.

"The usual?" Hill asked.

"Yeah, man, that and those thinking they are rockstars," Spank said. "Tough job being a valet in a big hotel."

Bennett nodded.

"I got to get back to work."

"So, you telling us to go to the Bellagio?" Hill asked.

"No," Spank said. "I said that we thought they might be heading to the Bellagio. I didn't say that they were there. I said, when I hear from one of my valets, I will tell you."

"Okay," Tip said. "We will come back and check in."

Tip turned on his heels and reached out and turned Bennett and Hill away from Spank. I studied Spank and smiled. I hesitated and studied Spank for a long moment before turning around.

Chapter 10.

"Okay," Tip said, with a casualness that belied the situation. "I don't know about any of you, but I say we go to Yardbirds, it is one of my favorite restaurants here and has great food," Tip said. "We should call Shay and tell her to meet us there." He paused.

"I could eat," Bennett said.

Hill nodded. He fished out his phone and texted Shay.

"I texted Shay. Told her we were on our way to Yardbirds."

Bennett nodded.

Tip nodded and led the way. We walked into the Venetian. We crossed the casino to the restaurant. I walked looking at the people gambling at tables, machines and various other game tables. The security guards watched as we cut across the casino and found ourselves at the clean and swank Yardbirds. There was a line.

Tip raised a finger and pointed to the hostess standing at the entry to the restaurant. He raised a hand and the hostess smiled, seeing Tip.

Tip stood in the back of the line and after a moment walked to the exit and entered the restaurant with us following.

"Tip, good to see you," the hostess said. She was an attractive woman dressed in a light blue blouse, dark blue trousers and leather shoes. Her shoulder length blonde hair was pulled back into ponytail. She had greenish catlike eyes, a straight thin nose above her thin lips. She wore no jewelry and had angular features.

"Asta, you are looking lovely as ever," Tip said.

"Thank you," Asta, the hostess said. "How many? Four?"

"No, five," Tip said.

She looked around the busy restaurant and nodded. "Give me one minute," Asta said.

In two or three minutes we were seated at a table with a waitress named: Monica. Monica was a spitfire. She was short and wide of hip. Her hair was short and close cropped to her round head. She had thin eyebrows above her blue eyes, slightly crooked nose and thin lips. Monica looked like she was thirty or forty but seemed full of energy.

Tip ordered the Charcuterie Board of Newsoms ham, Wagyu jalapeno cheddar sausage, pimento cheese, Salume and truffle tremor as an appetizer while we waited for Shay to arrive. We all ordered drinks. Bennett ordered an El Charro and everyone else did as well. When Shay showed up, she ordered Blackberry Bourbon Lemonade. I ordered an Old-Fashioned strawberry lemonade.

"So, Cam, you get to Vegas often?" Tip asked.

"No, not too often," I said.

"Most people that live in Las Vegas don't come to the Strip too often," Tip said. "It's a fact. The locals avoid the Strip."

For dinner I ordered a Butter Lettuce & Mango Salad, Chicken and Waffles with Classic Buttermilk Biscuits. Bennett ordered a Southern Caesar Salad, Lewellyn's Fine Fried Chicken and Skillet Cornbread. Shay ordered Butter Lettuce & Mango Salad, Lemon Rosemary Rotisserie Chicken and Crispy Brussels. Tip ordered the Sweet Tea Braised Short Ribs and Mashed Potatoes. Hill ordered the Steak Frites and Grilled Asparagus. He also ordered Southern Street Corn with his meal.

When the food arrived, the table fell silent. Everyone seemed hungry. beside Bennett. Tip and Hill were thinking and laughing and talking.

My mom had taught me to eat my salad first and then everything else. So, I ate my Butter Lettuce & Mango Salad and was pleasantly surprised that the salad had char-grilled mango, smoked pecans, tomatoes, onions and with a benne dressing. The salad was sweet and tangy and a surprisingly enjoyable salad. The chicken and waffle were a delight as well. The Vermont sharp cheddar waffle was a treat. I had to admit that I had never had a cheese waffle. By the time I tried to eat the Classic Buttermilk Biscuits I was filling up.

"Anybody want my biscuits?"

Hill had a healthy appetite. He finished his Steak Frites and Grilled Asparagus and scooped up the two biscuits I had left and gobbled two of them down before I had finished my first biscuit.

"Watch your hands Cam," Bennett said. "Hill is an eating machine."

"I think he is part goat," Tip said.

Shay laughed. I laughed as well. Bennett smiled at the lightheartedness.

Bennett made eye contact with Monica the waitress and got the bill. Tip threw down a hundred and so did Hill. Bennett and Shay climbed to their feet. I followed suit. Tip and Hill were the last to climb to their feet.

"Thank you," Monica said, with a smile. "Come again."

As Tip left Yardbirds he got the attention of Asta and tapped his heart and blew the hostess a kiss. Asta smiled and waved to Tip as he left the restaurant area of the Venetian.

"So, we heading back to Spank?"

"Yeah," Bennett said. "Cam you and Shay head to the Caddy and meet us in front. Hopefully, we'll have some good news."

Hill pulled his phone out of his pocket and reached out to Bennett.

"We have some good news, as you speak," Hill said. "Garibaldi is at the MGM Grand right now and willing to meet with you and me, if you are up for it."

"Okay, still going with the plan," Bennett said. "Shay, you and Cam, go get the Caddy. Meet us in front. Hill, tell Garibaldi we'll meet him in thirty minutes. Hopefully, Spank has some good news as well."

Shay placed a hand on my shoulder and as Bennett, Hill and Tip walked toward the hotel lobby we detoured toward the parking exit.

"So, what's next?"

Shay looked down at me and I realized how tall she was. Shay was easily a foot taller than me.

"I suppose, we follow the leads and hope to find your girl," Shay said as we reached the sliding doors to the parking area. The two doors slid open, and the heat of the desert flashed against my skin. The heat, even at night, was like opening an oven door and then walking inside the oven. The air-conditioned air of the casinos and all the interiors of most buildings created a false sense of cool that the desert tore away when out of those controlled areas.

I took a breath as the heat slammed down upon us and Shay scanned the parking lot for the Escalade. I scanned the parking lot too, but in scanning saw at least half a dozen SUVs that could have been our Escalade. Shay walked to the left and along the side of the hotel. I followed.

In the uncovered parking lot, which was on the eastern side of the covered parking structure sat was badly parked Escalade near a No Parking spot. The nose of the Escalade poked out, just a little, toward the No Parking spot.

I looked at Shay when I realized that she had parked the Escalade do sloppily.

"What?" Shay asked, with a smile. "There are going to be a dozen black Escalades in every parking lot in Las Vegas, the exact same year as ours," Shay said. "The only way to distinguish ours is to make it stand out, just a little."

"You did that on purpose?"

Shay exhaled and nodded. She walked to the Escalade and unlocked the door. Shay climbed into the front. I climbed into the seat behind the passenger seat. Shay turned the key in the ignition and the SUV's engine roared to life. I buckled up and thought about all that had happened since my arrival in Las Vegas.

The Escalade rolled out of the parking lot and to the exit. Shay found Las Vegas Boulevard and turned the Cadillac back toward the entrance of the Venetian.

"Here we go again," I said from the backseat of the Escalade.

"Hopefully, we make a little more progress," Shay said pulling into the circular driveway and looking for Bennett, Hill and Tip. Once in the circular driveway of the Venetian I craned my neck to spot Bennett or the others.

Surprisingly, I found Bennett and Hill standing at the far end of the driveway with Tip and the tall and talkative Spank. Spank seeing the Escalade nodded and jogged back toward the entrance of the hotel.

Shay stopped the Cadillac and unlocked the doors for the three to climb in. Bennett and Hill climbed into the SUV. Tip was the last to climb into the Escalade. Again, I found myself sandwiched between Tip and Hill.

"So?"

"We're headed for the MGM first," Bennett said. "Hill and I need to talk to Garibaldi. Then we head back to the Venetian and hopefully we find out some useful information."

The last comment seemed to be directed at Tip. I looked at Tip from the corner of my eye and the incredibly confident man seemed a little less energetic, if that was possible. I looked to the left, again out of the corner of my eye, to check Hill's expression. The musclebound Hill seemed the same unsmiling and serious individual I had met earlier that day.

Shay put the Escalade in gear and nosed the big SUV toward Las Vegas Boulevard.

The traffic on Las Vegas Boulevard was getting heavier as more people decided to drive up and down the Strip.

The drive from the Venetian to the MGM in the Escalade took nearly fifteen minutes. The traffic had become bumper-to-bumper for some reason. There were cameras and lights along the Strip as we drove. Groups of people were lined up on the streets watching something. I could not see what was happening, but I could see that it was in front of or near Aria. We could have walked there faster, I thought.

"Think they are filming some movie," Tip said.

I shook my head at the idea. Vegas was always doing something to keep Vegas in the minds of tourists.

The MGM Grand appeared just ahead of us, and Shay signaled, and lane changed and pulled into the circular driveway. The extra wide driveway had a blue Aston Martin parked and unloading a dark-haired woman in a yellow skirt. Next to the Aston Martin was an orange Lamborghini with black leather interior. Parked behind the Lamborghini was a GMC Yukon which was unloading three children, a woman with short blonde hair and dressed in leggings and a pink long sleeved top. The driver, a salt and pepper haired man with a mustache and shadow of a beard was climbing from underneath the steering wheel.

Shay stayed in the far lane and pushed past the three cars to the far side of the main entrance. Bennett pointed to the curb and Shay pulled over just a few yards from the entrance.

"Can I come along?"

"Naw, kid, this ain't no kiddie game we're playing right now," Hill said.

I looked to Bennett. He shook his head.

"We ain't babysitting right now," Bennett said.

"Next time," Tip said, patting me on the shoulder and walking to the entrance of the MGM.

I frowned.

Tip, Hill and Bennett climbed out of the SUV and went to find Antonio Garibaldi.

"What you think this? A field trip?" Shay asked.

"No," I said.

"This is real deal," Shay said.

"I know that," I said.

"Do you?" Shay asked.

I nodded.

"Some of these people are not nice and friendly," Shay said. She tightened her lips, thinking. "I don't know if you need to be around all the bad of Las Vegas," Shay said.

I chuckled.

Shay didn't say anything. I looked at her and then out the window at the cars parked near the entrance to MGM Grand. There was a Ferrari there all red and leathery and expensive. There was a Bentley convertible. Ahead of the Bentley was a dark black Rolls Royce.

Shay and I sat in the Escalade and waited.

"You want to listen to some music?"

"I don't mind," I said.

The music Shay picked was R&B. The Escalade speakers pumped out the sound of a horn and then the clear and siren like voice of a woman singing about being a "Smooth Operator." I listened and enjoyed the music. The woman had a good voice.

Shay's head bobbed to the music. I smiled at her enjoying the music. Perhaps, I smiled too much or tried to imitate her groove and Shay saw me. She stopped and looked at me for the first time as if she could pull my arms off my body like a toy doll.

"What?" I asked.

Shay simply stared.

"I can't enjoy the music?" Shay asked with a little smile.

I smiled. Shay was old, maybe thirty and in all the time I had been with her and Bennett I had to admit it shocked me to imagine Shay having fun. I couldn't imagine anyone except Tip going out and having fun.

Shay turned the music down a little more and shook her head.

"So, do you ever get involved in the talking to people part of the job?" I asked.

"All the time," Shay said with a smile. "I'm actually sort of glad not to have to talk to people tonight," Shay said. She quickly added, "You aren't included in that."

I nodded.

"The hardest part about asking people things is deciding how much they are lying," Shay said.

"You think everyone lies?"

"I do," Shay said. "It's in our nature."

I listened and didn't agree.

"I know some honest people," Shay continued. "Everyone likes to put their best foot forward. So, they indirectly or directly lie. It's natural."

"I don't agree," I said, despite trying not to be disagreeable.

"No? Well, you don't know me. I don't know you more than the handful of hours we have been together, and I guarantee you have lied about something big or small. It is just what we do," Shay said.

I tried to think about what Shay said. Had I lied? Were there times in the short period of knowing Shay that I had lied?

"Do you lie?"

"I'm human," Shay said.

"Does Mister Bennett lie?"

"Again, he's human," Shay said.

I smiled.

"So, if I tell you I like talking to you, right now," I said. "Am I lying?"

"Well, in the short time I have been with you Cam you don't seem to be a pathological liar," Shay said. "Now there are a few pathological liars who lie all the time, but they are rare. The typical person that is trying to have a good life, maybe get married, buy a house and have a job lies to cover up things. Hide things. They aren't pathological. A pathological liar lies like breathing." Shay stopped and looked through me and behind. "So, I would say that you aren't lying."

"Okay, if everyone lies then how do you know when they are telling the truth?"

"Well, the way I see it the question isn't to figure out when they are telling the truth. It is trying to figure out when they are lying," Shay said. "So, you ask something that no one would lie about and then see how they respond. That's the benchmark for me. Then everything is built upon that," Shay said. She smiled and allowed a grin to remain on her lineless face. "You have to know that people are going to lie about touchy topics. So, death, politics, sex or relationships are hot button topics."

I listened, not convinced. I knew that Shay believed the words coming out of her mouth. A question came to mind.

"Wait," I said, leaning forward. "If you think that everyone lies then are they lying when they tell the truth?"

Shay thought about the question.

"Have you ever heard of the liar and the honest man riddle?"

I had not.

"Well, there was this story I heard about when I was younger. It was a riddle. I loved it. It always made me think."

"Okay," I said, a little impatient.

"Okay," Shay said. "It's a riddle. Think about it before you answer it."

I nodded, suddenly interested in answering a riddle.

"You are walking on a road. Ahead of you, the road divides, one to the left and one to the right but you aren't sure which road to take. As you arrive at the divided paths you are met by two men. You know that one man always tells the truth and the other always lies. The problem is that you don't know which is which. You are allowed to only ask one question, and you want to know which path to take." Shay paused and smiled. "What question should you ask and to which man?"

I looked back and saw Bennett, Tip and Hill walking back to the Escalade. They were talking to each other. Tip shook his head. Hill smiled. Bennett became quiet as he approached the Cadillac SUV.

The three men climbed into the leather interior of the SUV that could seat eight people comfortably.

"I wish that I had better news," Tip said.

"This is a bit of a run around," Hill said to Tip.

"It is the nature of the beast," Tip said.

"I am amazed that you get anything done dealing with these people," Hill said.

"I didn't know we were going to deal with a Guido," Tip said. "I usually avoid them like the Russians who show up with a lot of cash." Tip paused. "They are nothing but trouble."

"Well, thanks for nothing," Hill said over me.

Bennett sat and waited for Hill and Tip to end their back and forth before speaking.

"We're heading back to the Venetian," Bennett said. He looked at Hill. Hill nodded.

"Spank texted," Hill said.

"What about Garibaldi?" Shay asked.

"He definitely is a lowlife and someone you cannot trust, but he and his people are focused on the redevelopment of Las Vegas. They have plans," Tip said. "But they aren't really concerned about Hudson or what they see as second or third-tier competition."

"The balls on that guy," Tip said, through gritted teeth. "He didn't expect to have a sit down with three eggplants. You could tell."

Hill shook his head.

"That guy is the reason I don't deal with the Guidos," Tip said. He shook his head and looked at Bennett. "They still act like this is 1940 Las Vegas or something."

"Easy," Hill said.

"I was surprised that you didn't want to jump across the table and strangle that arrogant bastard. The world has changed. There are a few of us with enough capital to buy and sell things even here in Sin City."

Bennett looked into the rearview mirror. Hill looked at Bennett in the rearview. I looked up and saw Bennett looking sternly in the rearview. Tip finally averted his eyes and quieted.

"He was a dead end," Bennett said. "Like Tip said, the Guidos have their fingers in a bunch of pies, but they aren't interested in Henderson. They seem to be only concentrating on the big dollars in Vegas, for now."

"Yeah, they could give two fucks about what's happening in Henderson," Tip said.

I looked at Tip and then Bennett. Bennett turned his head to see Tip. Tip seeing Bennett again checked himself. He raised his hands in surrender.

"I'm sorry, Lou," Tip said. "I just hate the condescending attitude of that... Guido. I mean, he doesn't know us from Adam, and he talked to us like we were wasting his time." Tip paused. "I'm just irritated."

"Why you irritated?" Hill asked. "That's how they are. They more than ready to take our money and use our labor but they don't want to consider us their equals."

"Is that just the Guidos?"

"It's everyone not working with us for whatever reason," Hill said.

"Okay, now that you are educated on race in America, can we find Kyla before things go off the rails?"

Tip nodded. Hill nodded.

"So, we have to concentrate on Wander Brewer and Cyril Paulson. Before we do," Bennett said, watching the rear of the Cadillac through the rearview. "We need to go back to the Venetian."

Shay nodded. She put the Escalade into gear and steered the SUV toward Las Vegas Boulevard. The traffic was still building. The light traffic had vanished replaced by cars, taxis, vans and tourist buses. People were dressed to impress and walking on the Strip as Shay steered the Escalade back to the Venetian.

Two suspects. Two dead ends, I thought. David Charlotte was a bust. According to Hill and Bennett Charlotte was a guppy with aspirations of being a shark. He was a low-rent realtor with high expectations but no real way to see through his threats. Charlotte, according to Hill, had money but not enough money to afford some guys on payroll to shadow Kyla and wait for the opportunity to present itself for her to be snatched. Charlotte was renting an office in a building off-off the Strip. He was a goldfish in a fishbowl and not a shark.

Whoever we were looking for had to have money and power. He had to be connected to money and power. The person we were looking for would be someone who had no qualms about stepping outside the law to get what he wanted.

So, of course, Antonio Garibaldi seemed to be the most likely. He was a Guido. He was somehow connected to the mob and the mob for all the FBI and Nevada Gaming Commission had done to run them out had run them out only to have them come back again under the guise of legitimate businesses. The dirty little secret of Sin City was the money that flowed through the city and the state was heavily mob handled.

Therefore, Antonio Garibaldi and the Brewer Collins Group seemed a perfect meeting of power and money. The real estate firm had not been around long but was involved in half a dozen million-dollar deals.

Yet, Antonio Garibaldi was a bust as well. Unlike Charlotte Garibaldi was a lamprey attached to a real shark, but the shark was not interested in Hudson or Henderson. The shark, the Brewer Collins Group, if it felt it was important was more than capable of seeing through a threat and kidnapping Kyla. According to Tip, Hill and Bennett Garibaldi did not know who Mister

Hudson was or care. Garibaldi had said in unkind words that Hudson did not merit the attention of the Brewer Collins Group.

With those realities in my head, I sat and tried to think about the fourth man that stood in the shadows as Kyla was snatched and I was beaten. I had seen the grainy picture of the man that Hill and Bennett thought was a part of the kidnapping.

The riddle flitted in front of me.

For a moment I thought about the other riddle that Bennett and Hill have posed to me. Was there a fourth person at the kidnapping?

I lean forward and hesitate. I touch Bennett's arm to get his attention. Bennett looks down and sees my hand on his arm. He looked back at me.

"Yes," Bennett said.

"I have been thinking about what you and Mister Hill said and I think... I am sure that you are wrong," I said.

"Wrong?"

"Yes. Earlier you and Hill showed us some grainy pictures of me and Kyla in the mall parking lot," I said, timidly. "You and Hill had a picture of someone out of focus and you decided that he was a part of the kidnapping."

"Yeah, I know that," Bennett said.

"Well, I am pretty sure that when I woke up in the security office, they said the same thing as I did," I said. "They watched the video." I paused and cleared my throat. "There was only three people that were involved. I think that fourth person just walked up or was in the wrong place at the wrong time and didn't help out."

Bennett looked at me for a long moment. Again, it was nearly impossible to read his facial expressions. I could not tell if he believed me or thought me insane. I waited.

Bennett nodded and looked at Hill. Hill looked at Bennett and shrugged his shoulders, uncertain.

"Maybe," Hill said.

"Maybe," Bennett said and nodded.

I smiled. A "Maybe" from Bennett said a lot and gave me a lot of confidence. At least, that is what I thought. While I was thinking how smart I was Shay's riddle flitted in front of my eyes again. I imagined Shay's riddle came to mind because I had just a small victory.

"You are walking on a road. Ahead of you, the road divides, one to the left and one to the right but you aren't sure which road to take. As you arrive at the divided paths you are met by two men. You know that one man always tells the truth and the other always lies. The problem is that you don't know which is which. You are allowed to only ask one question, and you want to know which path to take." Shay paused and smiled. "What question should you ask and to which man?"

Immediately, I think I want to know who the liar is and who is telling the truth. Then, as I think of that as my question, I rethink the idea. That doesn't get me to where I want to go. It is a good question if I have twenty questions, but I only have one question.

So, I think about the riddle again. Asking who the liar is seems logical, but it does not get me anywhere. I only have one question. I have to rethink the question.

I looked to Hill. The muscular man was looking at his cellphone. He seemed to be flipping through some pictures and a little distracted.

I turned my attention to Tip. The handsome and perfumed member of Bennett's group gifted with the ability to befriend most. Tip was adjusting his Versace ring when I looked at him.

Looking back at Hill I tried to think how he came to be a part of this group. Maybe he was in the military, I thought. I scratched that idea. He was the litigator of the group according to Destiny Salter, the assistant of Mister Hudson. A litigator was just a fancy word for lawyer. So, Hill was educated. He had passed the bar somewhere. He knew a few things.

As I was thinking where Hill passed his bar exam I came upon an idea. The idea was just a kernel at first. Then, the idea, grew.

I frowned at Hill and turned to look at Tip.

"What?"

"I was thinking that of the two people who are supposed to be in Henderson, weren't in Henderson, but checking on someone that was taken from Henderson it might lead us to... the someone," I said.

Tip nodded his head. He reached across my face and tapped Hill. Hill looked up.

"You got a number for Wander or Paulson?"

Hill frowned at the question. He looked down at his cellphone and closed the window he had opened and searched for one of the contacts.

"Hey, Lou, I think the kid might have a thought," Tip said from the rear of the car, directly behind Bennett.

"What is the idea?"

"Well, we struck out with Charlotte and Garibaldi and the Guidos," Tip said. "What if either Wander or Paulson are in Las Vegas right now? That might tell us a lot. Better yet, it might tell us where Kyla is," Tip said.

Bennett turned around in his seat and looked at me.

I smiled.

"Good thinking kid," Bennett said. Bennett looked at Tip who was smiling at the idea. He looked to Hill who was on the phone and had his notebook computer opened.

"Wander is in Henderson. He is out at some Battle of the Bands event in Henderson," Hill said.

"How do you know?"

Hill had Shay's laptop or someone's laptop on his lap. He turned his laptop around and I saw briefly this milk dud colored man wearing a leather jacket sticking his tongue out and raising an arm. In the background there was a band on stage with a guitarist near the edge of the stage. There were easily three or four hundred people caught cheering and dancing behind the oval-faced Wander Brett.

"That ain't fake?"

"I don't think so," Hill said. "This is on his business website, under Community Events."

"That don't mean it ain't fake."

"Well, this doesn't look like he put a bunch of effort into it. There are three or four other pictures of Wander in that same leather jacket at the same event," Hill said. "It's timestamped."

"Okay," Tip said, reluctantly.

Bennett studied the laptop. He nodded. Bennett turned back to the front, thinking.

"We are still headed to the Venetian, Shay," Bennett said to the driver.

"Got you," Shay said.

Hill turned the laptop back. He was still on the phone.

"No answer," Hill said. "I will call his partner."

"He has a partner?" Tip asked.

"He has three partners, according to the website," Hill said, again turning his laptop to Bennett. Bennett turned his head and looked at the laptop screen.

I caught the picture of a handful of people dressed in suits and ties looking important before Hill showed the screen to Bennett. The image reminded me of a movie poster I had seen of some gangster movie.

"Don't this look like some American Gangster type shit?" Hill asked, with a shake of his head.

"Yep," said Tip with a smile.

Tip fished out his phone.

"Which one is Cyril?"

Hill turned the laptop back and I got a better glimpse of the four well-dressed men caught walking on a street looking powerful and fashionable. One of the men with a bald head and well-trimmed beard was wearing a periwinkle blue shirt and bowtie and dark blue suit. Another man with a close-cropped haircut and square chin was wearing a Coke white collared shirt, gray checked tie and gray suit. The third man, who was a little bit a head of the others, was clean shaven, dark eyed, intense, wearing a white tuxedo jacket with black lapels, unbuttoned at the throat white collared shirt and black tuxedo pants. On his wrist was a diamond encrusted wristwatch. The last man in the image had a mustache and goatee. He had blockish features and seemed to be incredibly muscular compared to the others. He was wearing a white collared shirt, red and blue power tie and a blue three-piece suit.

Hill, once he flipped the computer back so that he could see, typed on the keyboard. He scanned the screen. In a few seconds Hill's expression went from nothing to less than nothing.

"Holy fuck," Hill said.

I looked at Hill surprised by his outburst.

"What the fuck is wrong with you?" Tip asked.

"Lou, you might want to stop the car," Hill said.

He flipped his laptop back so Bennet, Tip and I could see.

"This is Cyril Paulson," Hill said. He frowned at the realization.

I caught a good look at Cyril Paulson. He was the clean shaven, dark eyed man on the homepage wearing the white tuxedo jacket with the black lapels and the diamond encrusted wristwatch. He was a good-looking man in his early thirties with a broad nose and a slightly crooked smile. He looked like an older and better dressed version of Spank.

Bennett frowned as well. Tip frowned as well.

Bennett and Hill and I looked at Tip.

"Stop the car," Bennett said.

Instantly, Shay hit the brakes on the Escalade and though we were in the center lane of the Las Vegas Boulevard with hundreds of cars all around us the interior was suddenly eerily quiet. Car horns and people sounded off for the inconvenience the Escalade presented to those driving on Las Vegas Boulevard.

Shay sat unmoving.

Hill sat with his laptop in front of him.

Tip swallowed.

I watched Bennett sitting in the passenger seat, unconcerned about all that was happening outside of the Cadillac.

No one spoke.

I looked at Tip, who seemed to be the one in the backseat the most nervous.

Hill closed the laptop. He slipped it back into the sleeve and hid it in the back of the driver's seat back.

Cars streamed around the Escalade.

"You are walking on a road. Ahead of you, the road divides, one to the left and one to the right but you aren't sure which road to take. As you arrive at the divided paths you are met by two men. You know that one man always tells the truth and the other always lies. The problem is that you don't know which is which. You are allowed to only ask one question, and you want to know which path to take." Shay paused and smiled. *"What question should you ask and to which man?"*

Almost, without thought the answer comes to me. I smile.

Chapter 12.

The Venetian was one of two statuesque and distinctive golden structures surrounded by pools, an Expo Center and gondolas, recreating the city of Venice in the Las Vegas desert. Behind the Venetian was the Palazzo. Both structures touted the opulence and splendor of the Renaissance hotel and casino.

In the driveway to the front of the Venetian there was a covered run up to the hotel and casino. The valet station was at the hotel entrance. In the center of the circular driveway was a fountain. Some visitors were taking pictures in front of the fountain.

Tip, Hill and Bennett climbed out of the SUV. This time, Bennett did not immediately close the door, but looked back into the Escalade and at me.

"You coming?"

I was surprised by Bennett's question. I smiled at the unreadable man. I nodded. I also raised a finger, asking for a minute. Bennett nodded. He closed the door and the three waited just on the other side of the closed Escalade doors.

I lean forward and touch Shay on the arm.

She looks back briefly.

"You better go," Shay said. "They aren't used to waiting."

"I'm going," I said. "But I think I know the answer to the riddle now," I said.

"Are you sure?"

"I think so," I said.

"Okay," Shay said with a smile. "Tell it to me when you come back."

I push to the Cadillac door handle and pause.

"You going to be okay?" I asked.

"Yeah, kid, you watch your six," Shay said.

I nodded.

I opened the door and found Tip, Hill and Bennett waiting near the rear of the Escalade. I closed the Escalade's door and ran to catch up with Bennett and the others. Bennett walked casually, leisurely next to Hill.

Tip, the mouthpiece of the group, led the way. I fell in step with Bennett and Hill as Tip weaved through the handful of men and women standing in front of the hotel waiting for their cars or dropping their cars off and having someone bring in their luggage.

Bennett and Hill made their way gingerly through the men and women standing at the curbside of the hotel entrance. I followed along and noted the lack of children checking in or checking out at the hotel that night. It was late, I figured. It was nearly eight at night on a Thursday. Perhaps, I thought, families traveled on the weekend. Kids, younger kids, would show up Friday after school let out. At least, that was my thinking as I tried to keep up with Bennett and Hill.

Bennett and Hill stopped, just a few feet from Tip. Tip was engaged in a conversation with Spank. The conversation was animated.

Spank seeing Bennett and Hill nodded. He and Tip moved to our group.

"Hey, sorry it took so long," Spank began.

"I don't care about all that," Bennett said.

"Yeah, yeah, I feel you. I'm all about my business too," Spank said.

Bennett looked from Spank to Tip.

Tip nodded.

"Okay, Spank, before you say another word tell us do you know a Cyril Paulson?"

"Cyril Paulson?" Spank said. "Yeah, sure, he's my cousin. Why?"

"Why? Well, you know where your cousin is right now?"

Spank did not say anything.

Hill stepped forward. He looked at Spank like he wanted to strangle him.

"Look, Spank, we are looking for someone that your cousin might know," Tip said with a smile. "We are thinking that you know where your cousin and our girl are right now."

"Okay, first, I don't know nothing about your girl. I have been trying to help you Tip, you know that," Spank said. "I didn't try to squeeze you for cash." He paused and smiled. "You know that."

I listened and knew that Spank was lying. I looked at Bennett and knew that he knew Spank was lying. Hill had to know that Spank was lying. At the same moment, I had to believe that Tip knew Spank was lying as well.

Spank looked like he wanted to run. He looked left and right and smiled.

I watched Spank waiting for him to bolt. I wanted to warn Bennett, but I didn't know how. I imagined if I said something Spank would run. I wanted to say something, but I didn't. I figured I had time. I was with Bennett. He had to see what I saw. There was Hill, the musclebound tough guy who didn't miss anything. He had to know Spank was going to run. Well, there was also Tip. He was the closest person to Spank, and he had to know the valet was about to run.

Spank nodded to Tip and as Tip tried to defuse the situation the valet bolted. I had expected it. I had seen it in my head but that didn't stop my surprise. Even though I expected Spank to run but his decision to run, to turn and run as Tip reacted just a second too late as he tried to reach out and grab him. Spank was running almost full speed in three strides, which caught me off guard.

I initially took a step back. It was an instinct. I thought that Spank might have a gun for some reason, but he did not. He had just run.

Hill had stepped past Tip and was the first to run, then Tip and finally Bennett. I followed because I did not think to run back to Shay and the Escalade at that moment.

Everyone was in motion. We were all running and chasing Spank down the driveway. The valet ran toward Las Vegas Boulevard but then abruptly turned left and ran through a wide hallway of the casino and hotel. Behind him ran Hill, Tip and Bennett. I waved at Shay as I tried to catch up with the others.

Spank pounded down the hallway trying to avoid men and women and boys and girls heading to the main entrance of the Venetian. I tried to just use Bennett, Tip and Hill as my blockers as we followed the retreating Spank.

We turned right and ran past a LOVE sculpture and down a few stairs to the casino. On the left was a jewelry store and several armed guards. They were talking into walkie talkies and microphones as I raced past them. To the right, as we jogged left and right trying to avoid people, I saw the waterfall feature that ran at least fifty feet down the middle of the hallway to the casino.

Spank slammed through the opening sliding door and disappeared into the casino and hotel. Hill did not slow. Tip followed. I was on Bennett's heels.

Instantly, we were in a part of the property where security, guards and most of the gamblers resided. I slowed. I knew that being in a casino was always an exciting and nerve-wracking aspect of the place. Men and women were always sitting or standing and focused on the tables, machines and electronic tables. Some were smiling. Many were somber. It was a place of money and the possibility of money and all the emotions in between.

Dealers were usually standing and under the watchful eye of the table managers. Hostesses and managers walked the casino floor. Drinks and men and women hoping to win were everywhere.

I looked back and was not surprised to see half a dozen men dressed in a suit jackets and earpieces closing in on us. They were trying to not run and avoiding knocking down customers as they tried to close the distance between us.

I nearly ran into a pudgy woman with small eyes and curly gray hair wearing a I Heart NYC shirt and a fanny pack, but at the last second, I did a spin move like I had seen athletes do on the basketball court to avoid her. Bennett was just a few feet ahead of me. I watched as Spank ran beneath a sign that read: Mott 32.

The Asian restaurant was filled with customers as I ran in and followed Bennett, Tip and Hill. The hostess screamed as I shot past her in pursuit of Bennett and the others. Waiters and waitresses froze and watched as we zipped through the restaurant and toward the exit.

Spank slammed through the exit and onto Sands Avenue just on the other side of the door to the restaurant. Instantly, back in the night and on the Sands Avenue Spank took off toward the rear of the Venetian and away from Las Vegas Boulevard.

Hill, determined as ever, ran at Spank but seemed unable to close the distance between him and the valet. Tip, dressed in his silk pajamas and robe and slippers started to fade as we pushed through the dozens of people on Sands Avenue at that time of night. Bennett, seemingly recognizing that Hill and Tip were fading, kicked into another gear and motored past Tip. In seconds Bennett and I were passing Hill who was chugging along like a steam engine.

Spank turned right and ran parallel to the Sands Expo. The valet seemed to be trying to shake his pursuers. He had dropped Hill and Tip by the time Bennett and I tried to catch him on Koval Avenue.

Spank ran down the sidewalk looked left and then right and ran through a chain link fence bordered parking lot that let out on Paradise Road, the next street over from Koval. From a distance I could see the cars and trucks and buses moving up and down Paradise Road.

Once inside the chain link parking lot I watched as Spank slowed and looked back at Bennett and me. He slowed, tired, loping toward the far end of the parking lot and Paradise Road.

Even though I didn't want to give up, I wanted to give up. Spank was fast and like a gazelle for some reason. He was just faster than Bennett or me. I wouldn't quit. I couldn't quit. I had decided to see this through and if that meant running until I couldn't lift up my feet another step then so be it. Thankfully, it didn't get to that point.

From Paradise Road a dark SUV tore across the street, over the median and nearly sideswiped a sightseeing bus heading to Frontier Marketplace. Shay hit the brakes, allowed the bus to pass and then gunned the engine and turned the Escalade into the parking lot where Spank had run. The Escalade bounced onto the curb and into the parking lot.

Before Spank could get to the end of the parking lot's fenced perimeter Shay had slammed on the brakes and jumped out of the SUV.

Spank ran as fast as he could toward the space in the fencing bordering the parking lot hoping to escape by jumping the fence and avoiding Shay. Little did Spank know that the one-time basketball star was no slouch athletically.

Shay had parked the Escalade to stop Spank from easily exiting the parking lot. She closed the distance on Spank and as he hit the fence Shay slammed into him and driving him into the chain link.

Spank bounced off the fencing and crashed to the dirt and gravel beneath him. The long-limbed valet lay on the ground motionless for a moment, more stunned than hurt. Shay examined Spank as she stood over him and easily stepped on his right hand to make him know the chase was over. Shay reached in her pocket and pulled out a zip tie and restrained Spank.

Bennett slowed and I continued forward allowing my momentum to slow and stop beside the idling Escalade. Behind me came Bennett. Bennett pushed past me without a word. He was the first one to reach Shay and Spank.

Tip, out of breath, leaned against the Escalade. He was winded. Hill was sweating like he had just come from a sauna.

Shay and Bennett walked Spank back to the Escalade.

"What do we do with him?"

"Well, if this was a bad movie, we would torture him and then kill him," Hill said, breathlessly.

"We ain't got to do all that," Tip said. He wiped the sweat from his face. "All we got to do is threaten to tell all his peeps that he is a double-crossing, double-dealing rat and he will be through in Vegas before tonight becomes tomorrow."

Spank looked at Tip and Bennet and did not say anything.

"What you got to say?"

Spank didn't say anything. He simply shook his head.

I leaned close to Shay.

"Think you have to use the liar and honest man riddle," I said.

Shay looked at me and frowned. She looked back at Spank and nodded.

"Okay, I think we need to give Spank a choice," Shay said.

"What do you mean?"

"Okay," Shay said, looking at me and then Bennett. "All Tip has given Spank is the bad of the deal. What is the good? What does he get if he cooperates?"

Spank looked up at Shay as she finished.

"Yeah," Spank said.

Tip studied Spank and for the first time the friendly character seemed angry.

"If you help us and tell us where the girl is and we get her back we're done. That's it," Bennett said. "Tip will keep your name out of his mouth. We won't work with you anymore. You've burned that bridge, but we aren't going to go out of our way to bad mouth you unless someone asks."

Spank listened to the conditions offered by Bennett. Hill appeared still sweating.

"Okay, I guess that is the best I can get. I mean I did sort of get involved in my cousin's madness," Spank said, with his hands zip tied behind him. "So, the girl is at the Bellagio. My cousin is somewhere on the Strip. He knows I work at the Venetian. So, he avoids the Venetian and the Palazzo as a result." He paused. "Okay, when you get there ask for Cordell," Spank said. "He'll direct you." Spank paused by the Escalade. "You're going to have to make it worth his while." Spank paused. "You know we get by on the tips."

Bennett nodded. Tip seemed upset and betrayed.

"Thanks," Bennett said. Bennett opened the rear door of the Escalade. I climbed in first.

"You need to know that at least one of the bag men is armed," Spank said raising his zip tied hands to Bennett and Tip. Hill shook his head. "Maybe, if you find out I'm right and things are like I said you will reconsider things" Spank said as Hill climbed into the Escalade.

Bennett laughed and climbed into the Escalade.

Tip shook his head at Spank as Shay snapped out her pocketknife and cut the zip ties on Spank's wrists.

"Remember if you tell anyone and our girl gets hurt," Tip said through clenched teeth. "I am coming back looking for you, personally."

Shay climbed under the steering wheel of the Escalade.

I climbed into the rear of the SUV and the last person in was Tip.

"We're heading to the Bellagio."

Chapter 13.

Shay reversed the Escalade out of the darkened parking lot on Paradise Road and shifted into gear and drove away from Spank and headed north to Flamingo Boulevard. Bennett sat silently in the passenger seat, thinking. I watched as the leader of the group I was suddenly a part of closed his eyes and then looked back into the second row of seats. His eyes fell on me, then Hill and finally Tip.

I didn't know why Bennett was looking at me. His steady gaze made me feel uncomfortable. I tried not to squirm just as Mister Hudson had looked at me during the uncomfortable dinner, for a moment, and then Bennett looked at Hill.

Bennett, Shay and Hill seemed to have an unspoken rhythm about them that suggested they had been friends and working together for a very long time. As Bennett looked at Hill the musclebound man only chuckled and tilted his head gauging the other man.

The dark and serious Bennett stared at Tip evenly. He pursed his lips and as he did, I felt that Bennett was fighting his inner demons over how he was going to address Tip.

I watched for telltale signs of what was about to happen. Most adults' eyes hardened when they were angry. If not the eyes, I scanned Bennett, it would be in the corners of his mouth which told more than the words about to spew forth.

In examining the finder of lost things his eyes did not give away anything. In all the times I had been around Bennett I had not been able to read him or decide what emotion drove him.

When Bennett's eyes fell upon Tip, I saw Mister Bennett's jaw tighten just a little. The tightening was subtle. If I hadn't been looking at his profile, I might have missed the muscle's appearance. Mister Bennett was a man in control, usually.

"How did you get us mixed up with Spank?" Bennett asked Tip.

Hill looked to Tip. I leaned forward and looked at Tip.

"Before this he was rock solid," Tip said, with a smirk.

"Rock solid?" Bennett asked.

"Well, he was one hundred percent solid until this," Tip said.

"How you know him?" Hill asked.

"Just doing business in Sin City," Tip said.

"Is he going to turn on us?"

"I don't think so," Tip said. "He was solid up until this situation."

"Don't want to walk into an ambush," Bennett said.

"Not going to happen. Spank is about making some green. He is money-motivated," Tip said. "Threatening his income scared him. He ain't going to jeopardize that."

Bennett nodded. Again, I was uncertain if he was happy, sad, angry or nonplussed. He turned back and returned his attention to the road.

Hill and I looked at Tip and Tip shrugged his shoulders.

In the sudden quiet Tip looked to Hill and then back to Bennett, who suddenly was unconcerned about Tip or Hill or me.

"Credibility is the commerce of the street," Tip said in a low voice, as an explanation. "If you ain't got street cred then you don't get paid. We barter, negotiate and determine prices based on that street credibility. We have to be able to trust the information if the grapevine and the system is to be trusted."

"Who you talking to?" Hill asked.

I smiled at Hill's question. Tip fell silent next to Hill. I wanted to say something but chose to be quiet. So, as we drove, I found myself looking out the window and watching the tourists walk up and down the boulevard as we made our way down Las Vegas Boulevard and toward the Bellagio.

The Escalade turned on Flamingo Road and rolled up to Las Vegas Boulevard. At the Las Vegas Strip Shay turned the Cadillac left and made a couple of lane changes only to slow down and inch along toward the Bellagio. The SUV slowed to a crawl. For some reason there was bumper-to-bumper traffic. Friday Eve traffic in Las Vegas had ramped up and suddenly at a quarter to nine there was traffic everywhere.

The ride from the parking lot to the Bellagio, without traffic, shouldn't have taken more than ten minutes, but it took nearly double from the parking lot to the distinctive Bellagio driveway.

As Shay cut across traffic and pulled into the southern driveway and off Las Vegas Boulevard the Escalade nosedived as Shay found herself pressing the brakes hard to allow a group of visibly drunk women to cross the walkway. The group of women, all wearing Bridesmaids T-shirts, were weaving down the sidewalk and dragging a blonde, pear-shaped woman behind with a T-shirt and tiara. It was just a little after seven o'clock in the evening and all of the women were drunk.

Behind the Bridesmaids, just a few feet from them, a line of six or seven people crossing the driveway. There were two or three men and then a couple of men and women holding hands crossed before Shay was able to drive forward and into the Bellagio driveway. Shay expertly guided the Escalade into the Bellagio driveway.

To the right was the hotel and casino's tourist attraction. The Bellagio fountain was a tourist attraction in and of itself. According to Hill there were more than one thousand fountains swaying back and forth to music, lights and stretching more than one thousand feet and soaring as high as five hundred feet in the air.

"I like watching the fountains. It's one of those spots you take someone you like to check it out. It's one of the most complex fountains ever created and free. No matter how many times you see it there is always something different at each show," Hill said. "When we get your girl back you ought to take her to enjoy it. Guaranteed winner move," Hill said finally.

I knew that the fountain shows during the days were different than the shows during the night. I also knew that people stood around during the days and nights to watch the hourly fountain shows.

Shay pulled to the Bellagio entrance. A few hundred feet away from the entrance Bennett looked to Shay and said something that I could not hear. A few seconds later she stopped.

"We'll get out here," Bennett said, opening his passenger door and climbing out.

Hill reached out and tapped me. Tip opened his passenger door and climbed out. Hill followed Tip. I followed Hill.

Once in the driveway Bennett and Hill led the way across the driveway toward the entrance of the Bellagio.

Tip, Bennett and Hill walked up to the first valet who was closest to them. Tip pushed ahead and to the valet wearing a red jacket, white collared shirt, bow tie and black trousers.

Bennett slowed and let Tip do his job.

Hill placed a hand on my shoulder. He looked at me and while we waited explained a few things.

"Valets are all about money. They decide on how friendly they are based on money. No money? No smile. No money? No extra," Hill said. "They are the eyes and ears of the hotel," Hill added.

One of the valets seeing Tip smiled and spoke. "How can I help you, sir?"

"I'm looking for Cordell," Tip said.

The valet, studied us, and pointed to a thin kid with one of those nappy crowns of hair that is close shaved from the top of the ears to the nape. He was dark, with big eyes and smile.

"Can you tell him I need to see him?"

The valet smirked. He nodded.

"Cordell," he shouted. "Someone wants to see you."

The valet, who had shouted to Cordell, shrugged and returned his attention to the sedan pulling up.

When the first Bellagio valet departed Bennett and Hill stepped forward.

"What do we have?"

"He's on his way," Tip said.

I watched as Cordell, the valet, walked toward us.

Tip smiled and stepped forward.

"Cordell, Spank sent us," Tip said. "He said you might know where someone we're looking for is right now."

"Who are you looking for?"

Tip didn't answer the valet's question. Instead, he looked for a more private space.

"Is there somewhere we can talk out of the hearing of others?"

Cordell smiled.

"Why?"

"Look, here's a Franklin for just ten minutes of your time," Tip said, giving Cordell a hundred-dollar bill.

Cordell examined the bill he had been handed and nodded. The valet looked around and gestured to a door near the bell desk.

At the door Cordell turned around on Tip. Bennett and Hill were slow walking. As a result, I was slow walking and keeping pace with Bennett.

"Okay, here's your privacy."

"Okay," Tip said with a smile. "There was a couple of guys that came here with a girl wearing a Warriors basketball jersey and braids."

"Yeah, I remember them. There were three of them and the girl with the Warriors jersey," Cordell said.

"They check in here?" Tip asked.

Cordell nodded.

"We just need a room number," Tip said.

Cordell smiled and looked at Tip and Bennett.

"This is a high-class establishment," Cordell said, with a toothy grin. "We have a reputation to keep up. I'm not saying that I heard anything or saw anything. Because if I did see something or hear something I was supposed to report it to my supervisor." He paused, looking at me for a second and then back at Tip and Bennett. "So," Cordell said, with a smile. "Say if I had some information. How much would it be worth to you?"

"Well, the going rate on a room at the Bellagio is about two bills a night for the basic room," Tip said.

"Yeah, that's about right, if you want the run of the mill, average Joe, nobody rate," Cordell said, with a nod. "But you look like a high roller and the information, if I have it, isn't no nothing, anybody can tell you type of information. The better rooms are on the fountain side of the hotel. Now those rooms are pricey. People come here from all over the world to see the fountain show. So, you need to pay a higher price for those rooms and that show."

"How much for the fountain side of the hotel?"

"Six bills," Cordell said.

"Listen, we ain't staying overnight. We just need an hourly rate. So, let's meet somewhere in the middle. Say, three bills for good information. Remember if it's faulty, we expect a full refund."

Cordell nodded.

Tip peeled off two bills and handed them to the valet.

"They're in the Spa Tower. They are a little sketchy," Cordell said, then paused he looked at Bennett and Hill. "It looks like you know what you're walking into. I think there on the ninth floor. They checked into Room 933 or 935," Cordell added.

Tip tightened his lips. He was suddenly angry.

"What do you mean? 933 or 935?" Tip's lip was quavering with anger. "I just paid you for good information. Don't start getting funny style."

Cordell nodded. "Okay. They're in 933," he said with a smile. "But don't tell anyone I told you."

With the information from Cordell, Bennett, Hill, Tip and I walked into the lobby of the Bellagio. I had never been in the lobby. When I was in Vegas and on the Strip, I would just find the casino entrances and run through them looking for the arcades.

Going through the lobby, with the three men, I could not help but be impressed with the handblown glass ceiling that looked like flower blossoms of various colors. The glass ceiling stretched from the lobby all the way to the edge of the elevators and casino.

Bennett led the way to the elevators. Bennett had his phone in his hand. He was texting and typing from the moment Tip began talking to Cordell, the valet.

Bennett paused in front of the elevator bank.

"What's up?"

"The kidnappers have threatened to kill Kyla if we get the police involved," Bennett said.

Bennett entered the elevator bank. An elevator opened. Bennett climbed inside and pressed the elevator button.

The elevator climbed to the ninth floor.

"So, what do you think we're going to be facing?"

"I'm not sure," Bennett said.

"Well, we got to believe that they are well paid amateurs or minimum wage pros," Tip said. "From the video I saw they were stalking Kyla."

"Okay, so, maybe some wannabe pros?"

"Yeah, but they are in the Bellagio," Bennett said. "They ain't the smartest. They came here to lounge. They're not going to torture Kyla in the Bellagio. They are just holding her until they are told what to do next."

"So, you thinking they are bag men?" Hill asked.

"That's how I see it," Bennett said.

"So, how do we play it?" Tip asked.

"Get in and get out," Bennett said. "They just want to get paid," he added. "Nothing more."

On the ninth floor we all climbed out and Bennett stopped and turned back to Hill, Tip and me.

"Okay, according to the kid and Spank, there's at least one of these guys carrying," Bennett said. "Tip, you keep the kid safe. Hill and I got the room. If anything happens take the kid to the elevator and get to Shay."

"We got maybe five minutes... seven minutes tops after you start any commotion before hotel security comes up here and things get... complicated," Tip said.

"Got it," Bennett said.

The two men walked away from where Tip and I stood just at the beginning of the hallway where 933 sat.

"Just relax kid," Tip said. He looked back to the elevator and then down the hall Hill and Bennett were in.

My facial expressions must have given my emotions away.

"Don't worry," Tip said, with a smile. "This is the easy stuff. We just sit back and wait for them to the do their magic."

I opened my mouth to ask a question and closed it without a word. I turned my attention to Bennett and Hill as they found the door where they believed Kyla was being held.

Hill walked up to the hotel room door and Bennett positioned himself on the other side. Tip noticed that my attention was on the activity behind him. He turned as Hill knocked on the door.

"Housekeeping," Hill said, with a devilish smile.

Bennett nodded and rolled his shoulders back and forth in preparation for the action ahead. He bent slightly and waited.

The elevator bell behind us binged and I looked back to see the elevator door slide open. Out of the elevator emerged one of the three people I recognized who had jumped Kyla and me in the mall parking lot.

He was wearing a baseball jersey and a thick gold chain around his neck. On his wrist was the oversized watch. I narrowed my view, making certain that who I saw was the man who had punched me.

I froze and watched as the man who had punched and stomped me out came walking toward me carrying a bag from a fast-food restaurant in one hand and a drink container holding three drinks in the other.

Chapter 14.

I looked and saw the bent nose and lifted my hand and reached out to Tip as the man closed the distance between the elevator and us. The man did not seem to notice or recognize me immediately as I tapped Tip steadily looking at the man with the crooked nose and diamond earring.

Tip looked at me through his dark eyes and smirked, finding me touching his sleeve. He seemed angry and about to say something but stopped himself seeing my concerned look. His dark eyes looked at me questioningly.

"That's one of them," I said patting the silky clad fashion horse. Up close, I noticed that Tip had smooth skin and a diamond earring in his earlobe.

Tip smiled and nodded looking back to the nameless man walking toward us from the elevator. He nodded and looked back at me and bit his lower lip at my words.

"Gotcha," Tip said in a whisper. The perfumed, perfectly barbered dark man painted on a broad smile and turned around in the hotel hallway. He stepped in front of the man still wearing what he had worn hours ago.

I watched Tip and the approaching man and that oversized watch and a thick chain around his neck that was etched in my memory.

As he drew closer, I took in his U-shaped face, mustache and chipmunk cheeks. The dark brown man was older and bigger than I remembered.

I looked down and noticed that he was still wearing the Doc Marten boots he wore when he stomped me to sleep.

"Excuse me," Tip smiled, looking at the man in front of him. "What floor is the gym on?"

The man slowed, frowned and tried to walk past Tip. The man looked at Tip and then me and shook his head, scowling.

Tip frowned and without warning threw a right hook at the unsuspecting man. The man that sucker punched me seemed to be on guard as Tip swung with all his might and nearly caught him unaware. The man jumped out of the way and slammed into the hallway wall, spilling his fast food while evading the punch. On the hallway floor fell hamburgers, French fries and three drinks.

One of the drinks exploded and splashed on my leg. I jumped back as the two squared off in the hotel hallway.

"Sonuvabench," the bent nosed stranger said in a growl bouncing off the hall's wall ready for war.

Tip moved to close the distance between him and the bent nosed tough, his hands balled into fists. Tip moved like a dancer and seemed light on his feet. He did not seem jittery or afraid as he squared off with one of the kidnappers.

Instantly, the man pushed off the wall like he had been launched from a cannon. He placed one foot on the wall and used it to drive him toward Tip. The surprise attack startled Tip. He had not expected the bent nose thug to try to jump him.

Tip fended the nameless thug off. Tip found the thug had a handful of his silk robe. The two wrestled in the narrow hallway. Tip backed up and hit the wall. The kidnapper tried to circle and bounced off the hallway's wall as well.

I too backed up against the wall trying to avoid the fists and bodies that were suddenly flying around me.

I found myself trapped between the hotel room where Bennett and Hill had entered and the two fighting in the hallway. Behind the two brawling in the hallway was the four elevators leading to the lobby and eventual exit to the Escalade.

Tip and the bent nose kidnapper were locked in a heated stand off and as the fight seemed to stall, I decided to push past the two fighting in the hallway.

Yet, it seemed that seeing my movement the action reignited. I barely avoided getting punched by Tip and the kidnapper as I attempted to squeeze by both with thoughts now that it was better to be closer to where Bennet and Hill were.

Having avoided getting punched I tripped over an outstretched foot and fell headlong on the floor into the hallway. I pressed myself to my knees and was nearly on my feet when the weight of the nameless thug slammed into me, knocking me flat on the floor. The thug's weight knocked the breath out of me as he fell on top of me.

Before I could move, I felt someone step on my hand and then someone step on my leg and back and then without warning I was booted in the face and felt a raking across my jaw. The lancing pain in my jaw caused me to close my eyes and instinctually grab for my now bleeding jaw. Touching my jaw forced tears from my eyes. I tried not to cry but it was too late. The pain was intense.

Lying prone on the hallway floor was like sitting in a meat grinder. I tried to climb to my feet despite the pain. I pressed myself to my knees only to feel the heavy Doc Marten boot hit me on my side. I knew I had to get away from the fight I wasn't in. I crawled away, toward the room where Bennett and Hill were in, hoping to get away from the fight in the hallway.

I didn't get too far. Suddenly, the diamond earring kidnapper fell on top of me.

I blinked and tasted blood in my mouth. Before I could push the person off me or speak, I found Tip trying to pull me out from beneath the unconscious assailant. Tip had a cut lip for all his troubles. He pulled me up from tangle of limp legs of the now unconscious attacker and shook his head.

"Where were you going?"

He shook his head, not waiting for the answer. Tip leaned in and grabbed my chin, gently. He tilted my head left and right.

"How you get cut up?"

I winced, touching my jawline. I shook Tip's hand away from my chin. I looked at Tip and then my hand and the blood smeared on it from the touch as I tried to climb to my feet.

Tip breathed out a puff of air and shook his head. He looked at me looking at him.

"Never run toward a fight," Tip said, looking back at the still unmoving man on the floor in the hallway. "Second thing, never turn your back on someone meaning you harm."

I listened to Tip with a newfound respect. Upon meeting him I thought him a fop, at the very least and a preening fashion flip if nothing else. He had surprised me. Tip, with his perfume and immaculate look, in his dark blue silk T-shirt, robe and pajama bottoms looked like a little soft.

Of everyone I had been introduced to that night, he was the one I had not expected violence from him.

"Okay, we just hold down the fort until Bennett and Hill return," Tip said.

As he said those very words down the hall, the hotel room door opened and there was Hill and Bennett and Kyla.

My breath caught in my throat seeing Kyla. I wanted to run to her. I wanted the distance between us to be gone instantly. Tip seeing my reaction turned and saw Hill and Bennett and Kyla moving toward them.

I stepped forward and Tip reached out to grab me.

Behind Bennett and Hill came one of the three kidnappers stumbling from the hotel room. He was holding the side of his face and carrying a pistol. Behind him appeared the last member of the trio.

I pointed in the direction of Kyla and Hill. Bennett was already in motion. He spun on his heels and pushed Hill and Kyla forward away from the two men. Instantly, Bennett was cutting the distance between the man with the gun and himself.

Bennett grabbed the man with the gun and twisted his wrist and the gun went spinning out of his hand and into the air.

The pistol spun in the air and landed behind Bennett and the man halfway down the hallway. Bennett twisted the man's wrist forward and back and flipped him over his shoulder violently. When the man hit the floor, Bennett slammed a fist into his face as hard as he could.

Hill grabbed Kyla by the waist and ran forward across the twenty-five feet that separated Tip and me from her. There was no time for greetings, hugs, kisses or hellos as Hill pushed us back down the hallway over the unconscious kidnapper and toward the elevator.

"I got 'em," Tip said, letting Kyla and me move past him, and placing a hand on my shoulder.

"We're on the clock. Hotel security will be here any minute," Tip said.

"Got it," said Hill stopping and reversing course back down the hall toward Bennett and the two kidnappers.

I looked back only to see Hill crouched and running toward the fight Bennett was in.

Chapter 15.

I grabbed Kyla's hand and she and Tip ran down the hallway. We skidded to a stop at the elevators. I reached out and Kyla hugged me like I was life itself and I held onto her feeling the same way. I didn't want to let her go. She was crying and I was bleeding. We had to look awful, but none of that mattered. I just held her. I listened to her crying and trying to talk but unable to understand anything she was saying. She was still beautiful and heart stopping gorgeous. She was disheveled but that was to be expected. I brushed her hair out of her face as we waited for the elevator to arrive. I took a deep breath and took in the familiar smell of bubblegum and honeysuckles. That familiar smell prompted me to speak.

"You, okay?"

Kyla didn't answer. Instead, she just hugged me tighter.

I knew it was a stupid question, but it was the only question that came to mind. I fell silent. The elevator arrived. We climbed aboard, with the prompting of Tip.

Tip held the elevator for a second. He looked out of the elevator door. That wait seemed incredibly long. I expected to see the kidnappers and the gun and all sorts of madness.

Kyla was trembling in my arms.

Suddenly, Bennett and Hill turned the corner and entered the elevator.

"We good?" Tip asked.

Bennett stood at the door breathing like a bull, ready to charge.

Hill had a cut on his cheek. Hill looked at Tip and nodded.

The elevator door closed.

I looked to everyone in the elevator.

Bennett looked a little jittery like he had been drinking super caffeinated coffee or something. His shirt was wrinkled and there was blood on one of the sleeves. Hill was balling and stretching his fingers looking at the elevator door, ready for a fight. The hoody was stretched out like someone had grabbed it from the rear and pulled hard. Tip was closest to the elevator door still looking like he had just woken up in those silk pajamas. Upon closer inspection I saw that his silk pajamas left shoulder had been torn in the fight earlier.

The elevator descended two or three floors before stopping. The elevator door opened, and everyone looked to the three people, two women and a child, looking to climb on the elevator. Hill and Tip glowered at the three people trying to get on the elevator with them.

"Take the next one," Tip said with a smile.

The elevator doors closed, and the elevator descended the last three floors to the lobby. In those last few floors Bennett seemed to gather himself. Hill too seemed to be less keyed up. Tip, of the three, seemed the most relaxed if that was a possibility in the situation.

"Okay, we don't stop," Bennett said as the elevator opened at the lobby. "Don't stop until Kyla gets to the SUV."

Bennett was trailing. Hill was on the casino side, shielding Kyla. Kyla and I moved hand in hand. Tip was guiding us.

People looked at us curiously, but no one approached us.

Kyla, as we climbed out of the elevator, looked up. Her big brown eyes were rimmed red from crying.

"You, okay?" I asked. Again, I knew it was a stupid question, but it was the only thing that came to mind.

Kyla was about to say something when her eyes darkened, and she looked at me strangely. I felt my eyebrows tighten and the furrow appear between my eyebrows.

She reached up with her small hand and touched my jaw.

"You got hurt?"

I smiled and shook her hand from my jaw, awkwardly.

"I'm fine," I said.

"You sure?"

Tip pushed us forward and instead of answering I looked back and in the direction, we had just come from. I turned back and kept moving forward. We were a few feet from the exit when I heard someone shout.

Bennett put his hand on my back and pushed me forward to and through the lobby exit.

The Cadillac Escalade was a welcome sight to see once we got out of the hotel. I smiled seeing the black SUV. Kyla held onto me. Hill was in front suddenly and opening the rear door for me and Kyla to climb in. Tip slowed at the side of the Escalade. Kyla and I climbed into the rear of the SUV. Louis Bennett stopped in front of the open rear passenger door.

"Everyone in one piece?"

I looked at Shay, the driver, and smiled, only to wince, feeling the cut on my jaw.

"You okay, Cam?"

I reached up and gently touched my jaw, wincing again.

"I could be better," I said.

Hill was standing just outside the SUV.

"I'll leave you here," Tip said. "You kids be good. Stay out of trouble."

Bennett and Tip hugged. The two separated.

"Lou, catch up with me this weekend. I'm staying here. I have some more business in Sin City," Tip said.

"Got you," Bennett said. The pair fist bumped, and Tip walked away.

Like Bennett, Tip and Hill fist bumped before Tip walked away.

Hill climbed into the SUV. Kyla squeezed over as Hill sat in the rear of the Escalade. He reached across Kyla and grabbed my face, seeing blood.

"You fighting again?" Hill asked. "You know you are no good at this."

"What? No. I got kicked in the hallway by one of those guys," I said.

"Kyla scoot over," Hill said, pulling me closer to him and simultaneously having Kyla climb into my lap. She smiled awkwardly finding herself in my lap.

"Sorry," Kyla said with a smile.

"It's okay," I said.

Bennett climbed into the SUV.

"Shay, let's go," Bennett said.

The SUV pulled away from the Bellagio and toward Las Vegas Boulevard.

Hill retrieved a bag from the rear of the Escalade.

"Looks like you got a nasty cut under your jaw," Hill said. "You trying to be a hero again?"

Kyla looked concern.

"You tried to save me?" Kyla asked.

I opened my mouth and chose not to respond.

"You the same kid that got stomped out earlier today?" Hill asked with a pout. Before I could respond, he added, "Someone needs to teach you how to fight. Can't win them all, but you shouldn't lose them all either," Hill said with a crooked grin.

I gave Hill a sidelong look because he was holding my head like an egg in his right hand. He sat making faces as he examined my cut. "You might want to think about a self-defense class, real soon."

I didn't respond to Hill's baiting.

He told me I had no broken bones, thankfully. Hill was wearing nitrile gloves and had a light attached to a headband on his head for light. He was a little heavy handed but effective and efficient. Hill cleaned up my cut. He bandaged my jaw. When he was done Hill patted me on the head like I was a puppy. There was a bunch of blood on the top third of my T-shirt.

"You'll be fine," Hill said as Bennett looked back into the rear of the Escalade at his god daughter.

"Kyla? You, okay?"

Kyla nodded.

"Kyla, tell me what they said," Bennett said, from the front of the SUV.

We were on the freeway and headed east and back to Henderson.

"What did you hear?"

"Not too much," Kyla said. "Once they grabbed me up, they drove us out of Henderson, they blindfolded me. They told me to stay quiet and that it would all be over soon." She paused, thinking. "I knew we weren't too far from Henderson. I figured we were in Vegas, but I didn't have any idea where until they locked me in the room in the Bellagio."

"Did you hear them talking to anyone?"

"They were talking to someone they called on the way to the Strip. I think it was their boss. Think there was one of them called: Billy who was the leader. He was the one on the phone. He called or the boss called, and they talked."

"Billy? Was he the leader of the kidnappers?"

"Yes. He was the one who decided to snatch me," Kyla said.

"Billy decided to snatch you?"

"Yeah, they were following us afterschool, he told his boss. They had been waiting for a chance to get me, I guess. They wanted to get me when I wasn't with my security."

Bennett had his phone out and was listening.

"Billy said that the boss greenlighted the snatch," Kyla said. "He wanted to teach my dad a lesson."

"A lesson?"

"Yeah, something to do with some property up near Railroad Pass," Kyla said. "Billy was a talker. Billy told the others that he couldn't believe their luck."

"Railroad Pass? What did they say about Railroad Pass?"

"I don't really know," Kyla said, holding my hand.

"Okay, Kyla, did they ever say the name of their boss? Did they ever say his name?"

Kyla did not answer.

"Think Kyla," Bennett said.

Kyla frowned, thinking.

"Did you ever hear David or Charlotte or Wander or Brett or Cyril or Paulson?"

He paused. He looked back into the rear of the Escalade. He placed a hand on the driver's seat and craned his neck to look at Kyla.

"I'm not sure," Kyla said.

"Think, Kyla," Bennett said. "This is important." He paused and smiled. "David? Charlotte? Wander? Brett?" He paused, adding, "Cyril? Paulson?"

"I think that last one was a name I heard," Kyla said.

"You sure?"

"I think so," Kyla said.

Bennett texted someone on his phone.

"Thank you, baby girl," Bennett said.

He looked in my direction. He narrowed his eyes and looked at Hill.

"How is he?"

"He's a little beaten up," Hill said, who had biceps the size of my waist. "But he'll be fine." Hill smiled and looked at Bennett and Shay. "He ain't going to win no beauty prize any time soon," Hill said peeling off the nitrile gloves and disposing of them in a medical kit he had between the two of us. "But it ain't his beauty Kyla loves. It's his personality."

Louis Bennett and Shay smiled and giggled as we continued driving toward Henderson.

"Shay, when we land and get some breathing space need you to do some research on Railroad Pass," Bennett said.

"What about me? You know I got skills," Hill said.

"You got skills," Bennett said with a smile. "But I want you to make sure that Cam is good and my little god daughter is fine. Concentrate on that."

I smiled at Bennett's words and immediately winced at the pain in my jaw.

I looked toward the front of the Cadillac and saw Shay smiling at me in the rearview mirror.

"Shay, you check on this Railroad Pass thing. I just want to know what some bag men were talking about."

Shay nodded and continued to drive.

In the rear of the Cadillac Kyla held my hand. Hill smiled at the action.

"You a doctor?" Kyla asked Hill.

"Me? No. I was a medic when I was in the Air Force," Hill said.

"He's thinks he's a comedian," Shay said from under the steering wheel. Bennett nodded, in agreement.

"I think I could make a living doing stand-up," Hill said, with a chuckle and grin.

He looked back at me with a small smile. He turned serious, reaching out a hand and placing it on my shoulder.

"Like I said, I was a medic in the Air Force," Hill said with a chuckle. "Just patch 'em up and get them back to the real doctors." He paused and added, "I'm good at fixing people up."

"I don't want to ask," Shay said as she drove toward Henderson. "But someone has to ask. How do we avoid having Kyla snatched again next week or next month?"

"Again, I think it's all going to be centered around Railroad Pass," Bennett said.

Chapter 16.

As we drove away from Las Vegas and toward Henderson I found Kyla leaning against my shoulder. She rested her head on my shoulder and though I was tired and beat up I tried to think about what I knew of Railroad Pass.

I lived in Henderson and all I knew about Henderson was that it was the city between Las Vegas and Lake Havisu. Lake Havisu was a giant lake where the young and rich went to enjoy watersports. The crazy part of Lake Havisu was all the boats, jet skis and wave runners there. I had been there a few times and hated how crowded it was. It was a scene all the time.

The rich and powerful loved going to Lake Havisu.

The young loved going to Lake Havisu because it wasn't Las Vegas. There wasn't all the gambling and hotels and casinos of Las Vegas at Lake Havisu.

Now, I thought about Lake Havisu as a retreat from the overly tourist heavy Las Vegas Strip. In my head, I knew that most locals who lived in Clark County, where Las Vegas was situated, did not live in Las Vegas. They lived outside of Las Vegas. That's where Henderson came in.

Henderson was where many locals lived who worked in Las Vegas. It was only about fifteen minutes away from the Strip. Like Lake Havisu Henderson was a retreat to the normal life that Las Vegas could not duplicate. Henderson was a small town in the middle of the Nevada desert that had schools, libraries, churches, movie theaters and malls that were not so high-end that people could not afford their products. If there was a Gucci store in Henderson it was because it was Guiseppi Gucci, the delicatessen owner had thought it would be funny to have a Gucci store in Henderson.

All that being said, I recalled that there had been a couple of newspaper articles about Railroad Pass being considered for development as a still undecided land development. There was a couple of city, town and county meetings about the land. If I recalled correctly, Railroad Pass was suggested as one hundred acres of possibility.

As we drove and got closer to Henderson I wondered if Railroad Pass could be the next big thing, a Lake Havisu without a lake. A getaway from Las Vegas and attempt at normalcy for those that did not want the glitz and glamour of Las Vegas.

It seemed that Las Vegas had been attempting to take the Sin out of Sin City for years, but it was still Sin City that attracted so many to its casinos and hotels. The residencies of top-level celebrities were a shallow attempt at keeping the fans or those top-tier celebrities entertained while others gambled and were engaged in the sins of Sin City.

Las Vegas tourism had shifted from the singular gambling siren to the entertainment, family entertainment, lifestyle experience that Las Vegas offered. The showgirls were downplayed. The gambling was downplayed from the usual ads before. Now, there were ads spotlighting singers who had five-year contracts with hotels and casinos.

So, I wondered was the fight to develop Railroad Pass somehow connected to the rise in interest in Hendeson? Was it possible that Railroad Pass, a thousand acres of unused land that ran to the Nevada mountains was not simply a piece of land that held all these possibilities for development.

"Mister Hill," I said tentatively, getting the musclebound litigator's attention.

Hill looked at me and tilted his head.

"You live in Henderson?"

"No, kid, I don't," Hill said.

"Where do you live?"

"I live in a pineapple under the sea," Hill said with a smile.

I shook my head.

"No, I live in Las Vegas," Hill said. "Why kid? You want to come over and hang with me now that we have spent a few hours together?"

"No, nothing like that," I said. I shook my head at Hill. He was a wild spirit. "I just wondered of the three of you if any of you live in Henderson?"

Hill puckered his lips, thinking. He shook his head. "None of us live in Henderson kid."

I nodded.

"Mister Bennett," I said, leaning forward just a little. Kyla adjusted to my new position and snuggled a little closer.

Bennett looked back and frowned seeing Kyla hugged up against me.

"Careful kid, that is my god daughter," Bennett said.

"Nothing going on here," I said. "I was thinking about what you said earlier," I said and paused.

Bennett studied me.

"What did I say earlier?"

"You were curious about Railroad Pass," I said.

"Yeah, yeah," Bennett said with a nod. "What of it?"

"Well, I was thinking about it, and I think I might know a little bit about it," I said.

Bennett smiled.

I waited.

"What do you know?"

I explained. Well, I gave him my idea of Lake Havisu.

When I finished Bennett did not react. He nodded and sat back in the passenger seat as Shay drove through the night toward Henderson.

Hill reached out and placed a hand on my arm, to get my attention.

I turned and looked at Hill.

Hill smiled and nodded.

I looked in the rearview mirror and Shay was smiling. I smiled seeing Shay smile.

"Lake Havisu?" Bennett asked no one as the Cadillac rolled through the desert and toward Henderson. "Lake Havisu," Bennett said and rubbed the side of his face. "Lake Havisu," Bennett said for the third time.

Chapter 17.

When the Escalade finally parked in the driveway of the Hudson mansion Mister and Missus Hudson were waiting along with about half a dozen others. At the sight of the Escalade Missus Hudson broke away from the group and ran to the SUV. Missus Hudson opened the rear passenger door and pulled open it to come to face-to-face with her daughter.

The reunion was heartfelt. There were tears and shrill words that I could not understand. Missus Hudson wrapped Kyla in her arms and took her from the Escalade.

I scooted out of the SUV behind Kyla. Everyone at the front of the mansion, who had waited for Kyla to climb out of the SUV, moved forward. The only one not to move was Mister Hudson. He watched as the others surrounded Kyla and her mother.

I stood beside the Escalade as Hill, Shay and Bennett exited the SUV. Shay looked back and gestured to me. I followed behind Bennett, Hill and Shay. As we approached the front of the house I looked to the left and saw my Volkswagen in the driveway. At the threshold to the Hudson home, I hesitated.

Shay looked at me a little confused.

"I think this is as good a time as any to tell you the answer to the riddle," I said.

Shay nodded.

"What question should you ask and to which man?"

"I ask: If I asked him which path to take, what would he say?"

"Hmmm," Shay hummed. She smiled. "Why?"

"Well, say that left is the correct path to go down. If I asked the honest man what the liar would say, then he will truthfully say that the liar would say to the right," I said.

"Continue," Shay said.

"If I asked the liar what the honest man would say was the correct path, then the liar will lie, and say that the honest man would say to the right." I paused and smiled. "So, they will both give the same answer and then I would take the other path."

"Very good," Shay said.

I smile. I am glad I figured out the riddle. Then I think about what the riddle means. I look to Shay and suddenly I am concerned.

"What do I do now?" I asked.

"What do you mean?" Shay asked.

"I mean, this is a kind of a personal thing. I mean, it's a family thing," I said, unsure. "I think that I might go."

"Hang on," Shay said. "Let everyone say thank you, before you go."

I listened. I wanted to go, but what Shay said made sense. Reluctantly, I followed.

We all walked into the mansion and the six security men and women who were there were smiling and happy to see Kyla back. Eddy, Lloyd Colson, the driver, and Larissa seemed the happiest of all the security to see Kyla returned unharmed.

Mister Hudson's personal assistant and lawyer and three of the family members from earlier in the day were there when we walked inside.

Curtis Beaumont stepped toward Bennett and the cagey fighter measured the lawyer as if he was about to battle.

Beaumont raised his hands in surrender and smiled.

"I have something for you, Mister Bennett, to show Mister Hudson's gratitude," the lawyer said with a crooked grin. Beaumont handed Bennett a white envelope.

After everyone had hugged and thanked god for Kyla's return Mister Hudson gestured and the security directed everyone into the house. It was a long train of family members who had assembled to greet Kyla back and thank Bennett for her safe return.

I slow walked into the house behind Shay, Hill and Bennett. I was in no hurry. I actually felt like a third wheel in this very personal affair. I wanted to leave, but Shay had given me an out. I was going to stay until everyone said: "Thank you." After the Thank Yous I planned on leaving.

Walking past the security and into the main part of the home and through the phalanx of security I paused behind the gathered in the main living area of the Hudson home. There were easily twenty people gathered to welcome Kyla back.

I knew Mister Hudson, his wife, Kyla and her aunt Nicole. The Hawaiian shirt strong guy was there, now wearing a dark blue polo shirt. The long-faced man with a broad nose and goatee who had been wearing a business suit was now dressed in a collared white shirt and blue suit jacket. His wife who was wearing her signature tennis bracelet was near Missus Hudson.

Mister Hudson and his wife presented their daughter to their family in attendance now. They all climbed to their feet and were kissing and hugging Kyla again.

"I don't want to say too much," Missus Hudson said, holding Kyla's hand as she spoke. "I just want to thank Lou for being a true friend and a friend ready to lend a hand when needed."

Mister Hudson standing at the fireplace pushed away, thoughtfully. He seemed to be gathering his thoughts.

"Our Kyla has been returned to us. Thank you, Lou. Our Kyla, our angel is back, and I cannot express in words how that feels. When I was informed that she was in the hands of kidnappers the first person I called was my dear friend, Lou Bennett. Lou and I go back a long way. He is a great friend. I love that he is called: "the finder of lost things." Anytime I have trouble I call on him." Mister Hudson paused. "Lou, you brought our angel back and you, in so doing, have thrown a rock in the lake of all our feelings that ripples out with her return."

I listened and did not know what Mister Hudson was talking about. He had lost me when he began to talk about throwing rocks in lakes and feelings rippling. I shook my head, feeling the bandage pull under my jaw with the effort. I placed my hand on the bandage under my jaw and winced, irritating the recently medicated wound.

As Mister Hudson continued to talk, I found myself trying to see how much pressure I could put on the bandage and tolerate. I closed my eyes at my limit and let my hand fall away from my jaw. The pain throbbed but was tolerable. Mister Hudson was concluding as I stopped torturing myself.

"I just am so glad to have people in my life I can trust completely when the chips are stacked against me," Mister Hudson said.

I looked from Mister Hudson to Shay and tried to get her attention. I wanted to know if I could go. Had I fulfilled my obligation?

Hill was all smiles. He was leaning against the back of a chair. Bennett was standing near the family. Shay and I were near the edge of the living room, beside Hill. Somehow, Hill had found a drink and was stirring it with his index finger. He smiled and looked to Shay.

"This is definitely better than reality TV, any day," Hill said, in a low voice. He scanned the room. He shook his head. "This is the part where they try and one up each other on why Kyla is important." Hill looked at Shay and then me and shook his head. "You think that they are trying to cement a place in the will?"

"Hill, you can't be that cynical," Shay said with a smirk.

"Why not? This zip code ain't about emotions. They are all about possessions," Hill said.

"This is their family, good, bad and all the awkwardness," Shay said.

"Yeah, I bet they are all trying to figure out who gets what if Hudson keels over," Hill said, laughing and leaning on his chair. Bennett broke away from the family and moved back to the edge of the living room with Hill and Shay.

Mister Hudson broke away from the family and made his way toward Bennett, Shay and Hill. Hill stopped laughing as Mister Hudson approached.

In the background, one of the women was talking about how she felt earlier, when she first heard about Kyla being kidnapped when Mister Hudson walked to Bennett and gave him a long hug.

"Thanks Lou," Mister Hudson said. He seemed on the verge of tears.

Bennett patted Mister Hudson on the back, awkwardly and nodded when the two separated.

Destiny Salter and Curtis Beaumont were there as well.

"I cannot thank you enough for returning my baby," Mister Hudson said.

"She's my god daughter too," Bennett said with a smile.

The two powerful men nodded and seemed very comfortable with one another.

Mister Hudson looked at the blood on Bennett's sleeve.

"Did you give as good as you got?"

"You know me," Bennett said with a smile.

Mister Hudson nodded.

I reached out and tapped Shay.

She turned.

I looked at her silently.

"Give it a minute," Shay said.

I nodded.

The two men stood, and Mister Hudson reached out and placed a hand on Bennett's shoulder.

Mister Hudson nodded and let his hand fall to his side.

One of the security members walked up and whispered something to Mister Hudson. Mister Hudson looked back into the gathering and nodded. The security member shrunk back out of sight.

"Everything okay?" Bennett asked.

"Yeah, Junior just arrived," Mister Hudson said, looking for his son and his wife in the group gathered in the living room.

Bennett looked back in the direction of the living room. He returned his vision to Mister Hudson.

"Where was he earlier?" Bennett asked.

"He said that he had some work to do, at the office. He got here as soon as he could," Mister Hudson said. He shook the question out of his thoughts. "Tell me how you got my little girl back."

"You know me, Hud," Bennett said, rubbing the back of his neck. "We tracked down the perps, thanks to the help of your girl's boyfriend, and when we narrowed down where they were we went in and imposed our will on them."

"Imposed your will?" Mister Hudson asked.

"Yeah, these guys were just the low-level members of the scheme," Bennett said. "They were waiting for their boss."

"Their boss?"

"Yeah, I didn't wait to see or talk too much about it once I saw Kyla," Bennett said. He paused. "You need to be aware that one of your rivals isn't playing nice."

"Yes. Yes. I understand that," Mister Hudson said.

"The people we took Kyla from were holding her and waiting to hand her off," Bennett said. "They fought to keep Kyla so that they would get cashed out."

"They tell you that?"

"Not in so many words," Bennett said, looking to Hill. Hill smiled and shook his head.

"How you know all this?"

"Kyla told us," Bennett said. "She also said that their boss had been watching her for a while, waiting for an opportunity to snatch her."

The two powerful men looked at each other for a moment. Mister Hudson nodded. Destiny Salter sat and took notes as the two talked.

"So, what now?"

Mister Hudson did not answer.

"Hud, what's your plan?"

Mister Hudson looked at Bennett but did not answer. Curtis Beaumont, the lawyer, dressed in a Coke white collared shirt, black and yellow silk bowtie and black trousers, was listening to the conversation intently.

"We are weighing our choices," Beaumont said to Bennett.

"So, what's next for you and your crew?" Mister Hudson asked with a small smile.

Curtis Beaumont smiled at Mister Hudson's response.

Bennett seemed confused about Mister Hudson's response.

"Are you heading back to Vegas and your warehouse? Or should I call it your clubhouse?" Mister Kyle Hudson asked with a smile.

"I can't say," Bennett said, narrowing his focus. "Hud, you and your family are targets. You need a plan," Bennett said seriously.

"You worrying too much, Lou," Mister Hudson said. "Right now, I want to just appreciate Ky being returned to us, thanks to you." Mister Hudson paused. He studied Bennett. Curtis Beaumont watched Bennett. Destiny Salter was attentive.

"Hud, you know this isn't over," Bennett said, concerned.

"Why would you say that?" Beaumont asked.

"Because Hud is powerful," Bennett said to the lawyer. "Power draws attention," he added.

Mister Hudson scoffed.

"I'm serious," Bennett said.

I was suddenly interested in the conversation.

"You know that this is just the beginning," Bennett said.

Hudson furrowed his brow, thinking.

"You know that Kyla suddenly has a target on her back, just like your wife and everyone the people behind this can get to," Bennett said.

"I'm not going to let fear rule me, Lou. You know me. I can't live my life in fear," Mister Hudson said.

"It's not just about you anymore Hud," Bennett said. "You have to think about your wife and your daughter... and your son."

Mister Hudson turned away from Bennett. Curtis Beaumont nodded to Mister Hudson. The two began to walk away and back toward the living room.

Bennett stepped forward and put a hand on Mister Hudson's bicep.

With the touch Mister Hudson spun around with his fists balled. He seemed ready to fight.

Bennett studied Mister Hudson silently.

"You going to fight me, Hud?"

Mister Hudson opened his fists and dropped his hands.

"You know I'm right," Bennett said.

Mister Hudson flexed his hands.

"You all riled up? For what?" Bennett asked. "You know that property that Kyla was talking about? That property called: Railroad Pass? It's going to be developed and you and your rivals are fighting over it," Bennett said. "You know that whoever you are bidding against ain't nice. But you know that already. Don't you?"

Mister Hudson did not respond.

"Don't you?"

"I do," Mister Hudson said.

"Is this really all about real estate?" I asked, suddenly angry.

Mister Hudson looked at me as if I was an annoying insect. I felt the eyes of everyone on me, suddenly.

"You know that it's not Kyla's fault that you are you," I said, without thought.

"You little--" Mister Hudson said through gritted teeth. Beaumont reached out and put a hand on Mister Hudson's shoulder.

"It's not worth it," Beaumont said.

"She didn't have a choice in her parents," I said, not believing that the words were coming from me.

Mister Hudson took a menacing step forward, angry. Curtis Beaumont looked shocked behind his bumblebee striped bowtie.

Bennett stepped between Mister Hudson, his lawyer and me. Destiny Salter stood with the action.

"Don't nobody come to my house and disrespect me," Hudson said through gritted teeth.

"I don't mean to be disrespectful, but this is the hard part of love," I said.

"Did you say love?"

"I did. When you love someone, you protect them even if you aren't some armed hired security guard," I said. "If you love someone you don't dangle them in front of your enemies to figure out who's your real enemies. You just protect them all the time. That's hard love," I said.

Shay put a hand on my shoulder. Hill shook his head.

"You need to chill out, little fella," Hill said in a whisper.

I stopped talking. I was still upset, but it didn't seem like Mister Hudson cared.

"I'd throw you out, but you just helped get my baby girl back and that is the only reason I'm allowing you to stay. If it was up to me I'd…," Mister Hudson trailed off and spun around on his heels and walked away from me.

Bennett stepped to Mister Hudson's side.

"So, how do we stop this from happening again, Hud? Who should we be talking to other than Cyril Paulson?"

Mister Hudson tried to glower at me, but Bennett stood in the way. Hill was suddenly by my side. Shay placed a hand on my shoulder.

"Focus, Hud," Bennett said.

Mister Hudson pursed his lips.

"So, you know who was behind this don't you?"

Mister Hudson did not respond.

"Hud, remember Kyla is my god daughter," Bennett said.

"I know that Lou. I picked you for a reason. You know me. You know what it's taken for me to get here."

"I do," Bennett said.

"Well, to be honest, Lou," Mister Hudson said, through gritted teeth. "I ain't the nicest. I can be a dick at times in business. I have stepped on a bunch of toes along the way. So, honestly, I'm not certain who's behind this." He paused. "I mean, I know there's Cyril Paulson, a bit of pond scum, and his group of thugs pretending to be realtors." He shook his head. "I guess there's Wander Brett and David Charlotte, maybe, but I don't put a lot of energy into the wannabes trying to take my crown."

"You know you ain't got no crown. Right?"

Mister Hudson smiled. The two laughed.

"So, you know your rivals, are coming for you," Bennett said.

Mister Hudson nodded, reluctantly.

"You think this is it? You think it's one and done?"

Mister Hudson shook his head.

"Okay, let me ask it a different way," Bennett said. "How do we stop this from happening again?" Mister Hudson did not speak. Instead, Mister Hudson pursed his lips, thinking.

"I think Beaumont gave you a list of suspects. I would start there, but I can't say if that is the right group or not," Mister Hudson said. "In business feelings get hurt. It's the cost of business."

At that moment Kyle Junior appeared behind Beaumont and Destiny. Mister Hudson seeing his son turned and gave him a hug. The two embraced and separated.

Beaumont stepped beside Mister Hudson and patted him on his shoulder. He smiled and placed a hand on Mister Hudson's shoulder.

"I got this," Beaumont said. He turned his attention to Bennett. "Mister Bennett, Mister Hudson wants to thank you for returning his daughter unharmed to the family. He cannot express his appreciation for the safe return of Kyla." Beaumont smiled. "Regarding future predictions and plans, we cannot say. We are not fortune tellers. We do not want to say that we are going to do this and not do that. As you probably can understand, with the return of Kyla, Mister Hudson needs to re-evaluate some matters."

"What *matters*?"

"I would not want to speak for Mister Hudson but suffice it to say that he and the family needs to just be given time to evaluate this situation," Curtis Beaumont said. "Give Mister Hudson and his family a little time to figure things out. You understand. He and I and his team will evaluate all the elements of the personal security."

<h1 style="text-align:center">Chapter 18.</h1>

With that Curtis Beaumont and his bowtie escorted Mister Hudson and Kyle Junior away. In the wake of the Hudson men's departure along with Curtis Beaumont the team of Bennett, Hill and Shay stood looking at each other, unsure what to do next. Bennett, unlike everyone else, seemed sure of his purpose. I studied the three around me. Shay placed a hand on my shoulder.

"Things are always sketchy once Bennett points out the truth," Shay said, in a voice a little louder than a whisper.

"You know all that we talked about in Vegas seems to be what we suspected," Hill said. "The kid's thinking might be right," Hill said turning to Bennet and Shay.

Shay looked at me and smirked.

"I should have left," I said to Shay. Shay and Hill chuckled. Bennett stepped forward and placed a heavy hand on my shoulder.

"Give him a little time to appreciate getting Kyla back and then I'll talk to him," Bennett said to me.

I looked at the dark man who had found Kyla in front of me. I had talked with Bennett a few times but there was always someone or something in between. Now, as he stood in front of me, standing over me, he was just six foot tall and maybe two hundred pounds. He was clean shaven, angular featured and possessed dark and piercing brown eyes. I marveled at the scar through his left eyebrow. I wanted to ask Bennett how he got his scar. It was unusual, but I chose not to say anything.

"You, good?"

I nodded.

"Shay, go and talk with Hudson's assistant about what I asked you earlier," Bennett said. "I wonder if what I am thinking is correct."

"What are you thinking?" Hill asked.

"Not yet," Bennett said. "Hill you hang," Bennett continued. "I want to ask Hud something."

Bennett turned and walked back into the living room and was stopped by security. I watched as the security tried to explain why they were stopping him. It seemed incredibly stupid suddenly.

Shay placed a hand on my shoulder, and she walked toward the kitchen, doing an end around the security to Hudson's assistant. Hill and I just stood and watched Shay and Bennett progress.

I turned to Hill and shook my head. Bennett was Mister Hudson's friend. He was also Kyla's god father. If he was getting braced things were starting to spin out of control. I looked back at Hill and took a breath.

"I think I'll leave," I said.

"Don't leave without saying goodbye to Shay or Bennett," Hill said.

"Things are getting weird," I said.

"This ain't weird," Hill said. "You ain't seen weird yet." Hill reached out and put a hand on my shoulder. "Just wait for Shay to return and then leave. That's good form."

I nodded. Hill's logic seemed sound.

Shay returned to us with Mister Hudson's assistant. They had been gone for about ten minutes.

When Shay returned Destiny Salter was with her. Destiny Salter seemed shaken.

"Everything okay?" Hill asked.

Destiny Salter shook her head as an answer.

"No," Shay said. She paused and looked around the mansion. "Where's Bennett?"

"I think talking to Hudson," Hill said.

"Thanks for everything," I said interrupting. "I'm going to go. I definitely will remember today."

"Stay out of trouble," Shay said, with a smile.

"Don't take any wooden nickels," Hill said, with a mischievous grin.

I shook my head and waved goodbye. I headed toward the front door.

I was near the door when one of the security members near the exit raised a hand and stopped me.

"Mister Cameron?"

"Yeah, that's me," I said to the security person at the door.

"The family wanted to see you before you leave, if you don't mind."

"Are you sure?"

The security member smirked.

I nodded.

The security member waited by the door. I looked back and saw Larissa headed toward me. I smiled, despite being tired of all the drama.

"Mister Cameron? Would you please follow me?"

"Hey, Larissa," I said, thinking as the tall security guard smiled at me.

She looked at me as if she was secretly thinking of ways to kill me.

"I have a question," I said.

The security guard nodded and waited her hands at her side.

"Do you have my car keys?"

Larissa smiled.

"Your keys are in the car. It's parked outside," Larissa said.

"Okay. Thanks," I said. "I'm tired and I think I've overstayed my welcome," I said to the security member.

She nodded. "I don't think it's going to be too long," Larissa said.

"I only want to be here for a few more minutes before I head home," I said.

She kept walking. She took me to the side room below the glassed-in conference room. The side room looked like a dining room. There was a wooden table with eight chairs around it. Two security members were posted at the entrance to the dining room.

Mister Hudson, his wife and Kyla were sitting at the dining room table when Larissa and I arrived.

The swarmy lawyer was absent. I scanned the security members looking for Eddy. I did not see his blockish head anywhere.

I smiled seeing Kyla, she had been cleaned up a bit. She was now dressed in soft nubby sweatshirt. Her face was scrubbed and cleaned of the tears and dirt. I smiled. She had that effect on me.

Mister Hudson looked at me and then Kyla. He did not smile. Missus Hudson smiled seeing me at the end of the dining room table.

"Sit down, Cam," Missus Hudson said.

The three Hudson's were seated at the far end of the table. I looked at the table and decided to walk to the side where Kyla was sitting. I sat close to her.

Mister Hudson watched, silently. Missus Hudson smiled, studying me approvingly.

"I was told you were leaving," Mister Hudson said. "I didn't want you to leave without you knowing how much I appreciate your help in bringing my daughter back to us," Mister Hudson said holding his daughter's hand. "Despite your feelings about me and my feelings about you."

I didn't speak. I listened. I looked from Kyla to her father and then to her mother, wordlessly. I looked back to Mister Hudson.

"Thank you, Cameron," Missus Hudson said, holding Kyla's hand.

I grinned, awkwardly.

Just then Curtis Beaumont appeared with Kyle Junior. The lawyer smiled at Mister Hudson and the family and then paused seeing me. Beaumont studied me coolly. Our eyes locked and for an instance I could tell he did not expect me to be there.

Kyle Junior sat down next to his mother.

"Thank you, Cameron, for your help today," Kyle Junior said with a nod.

"You're welcome," I said, looking away from the lawyer. Looking at Missus Hudson I found her amiable and friendly.

Mister Hudson was still the gruff and hard man I had seen earlier. He had changed very little.

"I know that you think you know me," Mister Hudson said. "It, your opinion, doesn't matter. All that matters is that Kyla and her mother know I love them. I love my family. They are why I do what I do. I am going to do whatever is necessary to protect them," Mister Hudson said.

I opened my mouth only to close it. I looked at Junior Hudson and noted the sting he felt in the obvious omission.

Beaumont sat at the table with the two Hudson men watching me like I was a piece of meat. I noted that Destiny Salter, Mister Hudson's assistant was missing from this intimate gathering and found it odd. She seemed to be everywhere Mister Hudson was. So, her absence was noticeable. I wondered if she was still with Shay and Bennett.

"You have questions?" Mister Hudson asked.

I shook my head.

"You seemed to be full of questions when you were with Bennett and his crew, just a moment ago," Mister Hudson said, with a scowl. He seemed to suddenly be a cat and I was his mouse he was playing with.

"Yes, I would be curious what you have to say now, about Kyla," Beaumont said with a greasy sneer.

Just then Bennett appeared with Shay, Destiny Salter and Hill. The security stopped the three. One of the security members spoke into their lapel. Instantly, two more security members appeared.

"I was just concerned about Kyla," I said, finally looking at Mister Hudson. "I mean, I care about her. I don't want her hurt. I don't want people to hurt her."

Missus Hudson nodded. Junior nodded. Beaumont, for the first time seemed to understand and even he nodded.

Mister Hudson burst out laughing. His laugh was surprising. It took me off guard. I might have jumped with the unexpected noise.

"Don't you think I understand all the threats circling me and my family? Do you think I'm some type of fool?"

I wasn't sure about the first question. In my head, it seemed that Mister Hudson thought that money could buy safety. I didn't know of any amount of money being able to do that. I didn't respond to that question. It seemed as if Mister Hudson was trying to make me insult him. So, I chose not to answer the second question.

I looked at Kyla's father and though he did seem foolish not accepting the advice of Bennett, who was I to say that. Again, in my head, I felt that Mister Hudson was looking for a way to throw me out of his home in front of his wife and Kyla.

"I didn't mean anything by that, sir," I said, in the form of an apology. "I just care about her, just like I care about anyone, and I don't want her kidnapped or whatever."

Missus Hudson smiled and placed a hand on her husband's forearm.

"Cameron, I am glad that you were there when my baby was snatched. I wish you were able to fight off the kidnappers," Mister Hudson said, with a chuckle.

"There were three of them, daddy," Kyla said, reminding her father of my disadvantage.

I nodded.

"One of them had a gun," Kyla said.

"I know all that," Mister Hudson said to Kyla. He turned and looked back at me. "My baby girl likes you," Mister Hudson said, continuing. "My wife likes you." He paused and swallowed. "I am finding it hard not to like you, myself, despite my gut feelings."

I watched Mister Hudson intently. At the corner of his lip there seemed a slow curling for just a moment. Mister Hudson looked at me and chuckled, not a full-throated chuckle but a light friendly chuckle. I smiled in that small victory.

"Well, sir, I am a likable kind of person," I said, grinning just a little.

Just then Kyla and Missus Hudson both giggled.

Kyla smiled. She shook her head at me. She looked at me and mouthed: You are such a goof.

I mouthed back: Your goof.

"Well, if you're going to be around my baby girl, you're going to have to learn how to defend yourself and protect my daughter."

I blanched.

"What you're not willing to protect my baby girl?" Mister Hudson asked, looking back and seeing Bennett and his team walking toward them. "Lou? What is going on?"

"Hud, I hate to be the one to tell you this but there's a snake in your garden," Bennett said as he approached.

Mister Hudson climbed to his feet. Curtis Beaumont too climbed to his feet, spinning to see Bennett and the three others moving to the table.

"Lou, this is *family business*," Mister Hudson said.

"Hud, the problem is that this," Bennett said, waving to everyone in the room. "This is *family business*," Bennett said, in reply.

Destiny Salter was standing beside Bennett with her notebook computer. She looked as if she had a bad stomachache. Her friendly smile was absent.

Mister Hudson looked at his personal assistant and scowled.

"Destiny? What is this about?"

"Well, sir, we have some troubling news," Destiny said. She looked at Mister Hudson and then back at Shay.

Hill stepped forward and smiled at Mister Hudson.

Hudson recoiled seeing the strong man.

"I'm Hill," Hill said. "We got some bad news, amigo."

"Lou," Hudson said, looking to Bennett. "Handle your people."

Bennett stepped forward and stretched his hand out to stop Hill from moving past him.

Everyone at the table suddenly seemed on edge.

"You know that we were recently in Las Vegas to find and retrieve my god daughter?" Bennett asked, not stopping to give anyone time to answer. "When we got there, we were surprised to find that there were a couple of people from Henderson in Las Vegas at the exact same time that my little Kyla was there." Bennett paused and studied the table. "There were only supposed to be two people from Henderson realty there. So, we checked on them." Bennett was at the head of the table. He slowly walked to the side of the table where Missus Hudson and Kyla were sitting.

"Two things surprised me. Cyril Paulson, a Henderson realtor, was in Las Vegas at the same hotel where Kyla was located. We learned that Cyril had put the whole kidnapping thing together," Bennett said. "Well, he put the wheels in motion. He had hoped to throw Kyle off his game in the Railroad Pass project planning." Bennett stopped and looked to Destiny Salter. "Destiny showed us the preliminary information on the project plan for Railroad Pass. The thing that is odd is that there were two projects submitted for consideration." Bennett looked at Junior Hudson coolly.

"What are you talking about?" Mister Hudson said.

Louis Bennett stopped and looked at everyone at the table and his eyes stopped when he found Junior Hudson. Junior Hudson climbed to his feet and stood beside his mother.

"I'm telling you that with a little digging we found out that the second approved project for Railroad Pass is a joint venture by Cyril Paulson and three others including Kyle Hudson Junior," Bennett said.

"What?" Mister Hudson asked.

Junior Hudson stepped forward and then backed away from his mother.

Mister Hudson spun around and looked at his son.

"Junior, is he telling me the truth?"

Junior Hudson smirked.

"You taught me to always think ahead," Junior Hudson said.

"Kyle," Missus Hudson said. She reached out for her son, and he waved her hand away.

Missus Hudson and Kyla stood up, stunned by the revelation. I stood, hearing Kyle Junior's name.

"What? You expected me to live under the threat of not getting anything?" Junior asked. "You want me to take your threats of bypassing me as heir apparent as jokes?" Junior Hudson asked stepping away from his mother boldly and looking at his father scornfully. "You threatened to cut me off when I fell in love with Jennifer."

"I had to be sure that you loved her," Mister Hudson said.

"It's your default setting. You threatened to disown me for marrying Jennifer," Junior said with a scowl. "You threatened to disown me and write me out of your will because you don't like that we live in Vegas." Junior stepped away from the table. "No one can live up to your expectations. More importantly, who would want to?" Kyle Junior asked with a smirk. "I hate how you chip away at my confidence every time I'm near you. Every time I come here... I feel attacked. I hate it here and it is why I only come here when invited." Kyle Junior paused and took a breath. "There I said it." He smiled. "When you started talking about cutting me out of the business and your will, I didn't take that as a threat. I took it as a promise. So, I created alliances, relationships, with some of your rivals to protect me and Jennifer," Junior Hudson said, with a sneer. He backed up and toward the rear of the dining room table.

"Junior," Missus Hudson said.

"Mom, it's okay," Junior said with a shake of his head. "I learned a lot being Kyle Hudson's son. I learned to think on my feet. If someone tries to steal something from me then I have to figure out a way to protect myself. Right? Isn't that right daddy?" Junior asked.

Mister Hudson didn't speak.

"I'm glad you know," Junior said. "I have been holding this in for a while. So, before I leave though, I just want to be clear. I love you all. I even love you dad. Just because I am thinking about my future doesn't mean that I was involved in what happened to Kyla," Junior Hudson said. "She's my sister. I would never knowingly allow her to be harmed."

"Wait, you knew about Paulson's plan to kidnap Kyla?"

"Well," Kyle Junior said, pausing. "No." Junior said. He paused. "I knew that he and the investors were planning on something big to secure the Railroad Pass property listings along with a dozen others while you were dealing with some personal issues."

"Junior," Missus Hudson said, shocked.

"Personal issues," Mister Hudson said.

"You taught me to focus on business and business only," Junior said, looking from his mother to his father. "What did you always tell me?" Junior asked his father. "Nothing personal. Strictly business."

Bennett and Hill closed in on Junior. Kyle Junior seeing the two men approaching, instinctively backed up and toward his father.

"Kay Jay, you also know I also said: If you aren't working with me then you must be working against me," Mister Hudson said.

"No. No. It's not that simple. Nothing is that simple," Junior Hudson said. He had reached the end of the dining table and found himself boxed in by a single security guard. Junior Hudson stretched his arms out and fended the guard off.

"You taught me to chase the money. If one avenue dries up, you said, there's another opportunity somewhere that someone else is sitting on that they don't know about," Junior Hudson said. He smirked. "I don't care that you think that I am weak. Or whatever. I suppose I am not mad at the idea of being second banana to you or mom," Junior said, looking to his parents. "That's normal. You're my parents. But I am not going to watch you threaten to give Kyla the empire because you don't think I have done enough to prove my worth."

Mister Hudson took a step toward his son.

"I have to make my decisions based on my future. Those decisions are for me and Jennifer's future since we are not a part of your future." Junior Hudson was struggling. "You raised me. You taught me to be ruthless. Now I have to make moves on my own," Junior said and stopped. "Good or bad."

"Junior," Mister Hudson said and went quiet. "Get out of my house."

Junior Hudson smirked and walked past the security member and out of the front door of the Hudson mansion.

After Junior Hudson left there was all this confusion. I reached out to Kyla and pulled her to the side as the adults argued amongst themselves.

"I'm leaving," I said.

Kyla looked confused and afraid.

"What? This is getting into some real family stuff," I said, fumbling. "I don't want to be in the middle of that."

"Don't go, just yet," Kyla said, and as she did, she squeezed my hand. The squeeze was not intense or urgent but emphasizing her desire for me to stay.

I was cut and bruised and tired and hurt but I stayed despite all the drama that was going on around me and Kyla. She inched toward me, and I held her as her father, mother and lawyer talked about what happened. I watched mutely as Bennett, Hill and Shay prepared to leave.

Destiny Salter, Mister Hudson's assistant, was the first of the bunch to bid her farewell.

"Kyla, you know, if you need anything, I am available," she said to the girl hugging me like I was a Teddy bear. Kyla didn't speak. She just nodded her head and clung to me.

Hill waved but did not stop to say goodbye. I waved goodbye to the musclebound comedian. Kyla hugged me tighter.

"I wish this was over," Kyla said into my chest. Secretly, or not so secretly, I too wished this whole night was over as well.

The next to say farewell was Curtis Beaumont with his bumblebee striped bowtie and smugness. He ignored me and concentrated his goodbye to Kyla.

"Kyla, I am leaving now. I have told your parents not to worry about Kyle Junior. I will be filing a restraining order against him and making sure that your safety is our highest priority. Your father has asked me to look into a number of options thanks to the insight of Mister Bennett," Beaumont said in his sing song fashion. He paused and smiled. "I don't want to bore you with the details. Just know that you are your father's greatest treasure." Beaumont smiled, bowed and turned on his heels and left the mansion.

"I don't like that guy," I said to Kyla.

She looked up with her big brown doe eyes and didn't say anything. She looked tired and worn out. She still looked like a magazine cover girl, but a tired one.

"I don't trust anyone that has to tell you they are being honest or that they care about something. Actions speak louder than words," I said.

Kyla squeezed me as an answer. I looked down and she looked up. I leaned down to kiss her only to be interrupted by Bennett and Shay.

"Hey," Bennett said. "Remember she is my god daughter. I am watching out for her."

"Don't listen to him, Cam," Shay said with a smile. "We're heading out. We got other things to do."

I smiled.

"Baby girl, if you need anything," Bennett said to Kyla. "Anything. You know I'm just a phone call away."

Kyla nodded.

"Good night," Shay said and turned on her heels and followed Bennett out of the front door.

With all the family gone and just a skeleton crew of security I looked at Kyla and shrugged my shoulders.

"I guess I'll be heading home now," I said.

Kyla was reluctant to let me go and honestly, I did not mind standing there in the middle of her home holding onto Kyla. She was beautiful. She was soft to the touch and as an added bonus she smelled incredibly good.

As I was trying to work up the courage to push Kyla away and head home her mother and father appeared. Missus Hudson was dressed as she had been earlier, a money green dress with a high buttoned throat and half sleeves, on her feet were blue and green slippers.

"Cam?" Missus Hudson asked, surprised to see me still in her home. "I thought you had left already."

"No ma'am," I said. "I was just getting ready to leave when you showed up." I smiled seeing Mister Hudson looking at me and deciding if I was the newest threat to his family.

Seeing her parents Kyla reluctantly and slowly released me.

"I'll see you in school tomorrow?" Kyla asked.

"Yep," I said.

"Okay, see you tomorrow," Kyla said.

I nodded and left the Hudson's home under the watchful and judgmental gaze of Mister Kyle Hudson, realtor.

Chapter 19.

By the time I drove home I was dog tired. I kissed my mom and grabbed something from the fridge and went to my room. I fell asleep and did not dream about anything. I think I was too tired to do anything but rest.

The next morning, I woke and still had the telltale bandage on my jaw from my adventure in Sin City. I climbed out of bed and wondered how I had made it back to Henderson in one piece.

All the things that happened on a Thursday were enough to fill a book. Listening to Kyla we had snuck to the mall and that one thing set the wheels in motion for a chaotic and incredibly memorable Thursday. I washed up and cleaned up and dressed. I thought about all the things that had happened yesterday and rubbed my eyes feeling the weight of all the events on my shoulders again.

I left the Hudson mansion last night with a headache. There was all this craziness about the Hudson home. Junior had been disowned or threatened to be disowned. He had told everyone that he was not coming back to the Hudson mansion even if his mother invited him. The lawyer, the smug SOB, was going to take some legal actions. The betrayal of the family circled the entire end of the night.

What was the betrayal over? Money? Power? The whole Railroad Pass project was suddenly a big deal. There was Cyril Paulson, the pond scum, and Kyle Hudson vying for the very valuable land development. There was also the ongoing issue of Kyla's safety and the safety of all the Hudson family, now minus Junior. I couldn't begin to pretend to understand all the levels of the Hudson's inner workings. Suffice it to say that for me all that I cared about was the seventeen-year-old stunner that some called Blue Ivy and others called Kyla and I called my girlfriend.

So, I texted Kyla as I was leaving for school. I didn't want to push, just wanted her to know I was thinking about her. She didn't respond. I didn't think too much of it.

I drove to Foothill High School and parked my car in the parking lot and headed into school. Before I entered, I checked my phone one last time only to find that Kyla had not responded to my text.

I walked the halls and before the bell saw a few friends in my first period class. I went through the first period class and then the second period class before homeroom. Homeroom was a twenty-five-minute check-in with our homeroom teacher who had followed us since Freshman year. My homeroom teacher was Miss Cole-Marshall. She was a friendly and knowledgeable teacher. She taught Math and was also the cheerleader coach. As a result, homeroom was always filled with Cole-Marshall's cheerleaders or potential cheerleaders discussing the endless issues of cheerleading.

Friday at Foothill High School there was a rumor that Kyla Hudson was leaving the school. I heard the rumors and by second period I was trying to find Kyla. I went through the first half of the day without seeing Kyla Hudson. By lunch I was desperate to find my girlfriend.

So, that day at lunch, I walked to the lunch table where her friends Morgan and Cindy sat and asked them about Kyla.

"How do you not know?" Cindy asked, rolling her big brown eyes.

"I thought she was your girlfriend?" Morgan asked pouting.

Wes, Justice and Lyle were no help. They were unimpressed with the whole Kyla relationship thing.

"What is going on?" Lyle asked with one of those pie-eating grins.

I hesitated. Lyle seemed to be circling me like a shark with his eyes.

"Is it true?" Wes asked. He leaned on my shoulder smelling of bubblegum and Axe cologne.

"Is what true?" Lyle asked.

"Heard that Blue Ivy transferred this morning," Wes said to Lyle.

I tried not to react.

"How come you don't know what's going on with your girl?" Lyle asked, reading my facial expression.

"What is going on, Cam?" Wes asked, curious.

"Your girl ghosted you?" Lyle asked with a smile.

I turned annoyed by Wes and Lyle delight in my misery. Just an arm's reach away I saw Justice sit down at the lunch table with his tray of food and apple juice.

"Is that true? The rumor has it that your girl transferred?" Lyle asked me. I shrugged my shoulders. In response, he rolled his eyes.

"Portia told Tracy that she saw your girl here this morning and that she was transferring or doing home schooling," Wes said. "I didn't believe them."

Lyle, eating his lunch, shook his head, disapprovingly.

"I wanted to ask you," Wes said. "I mean you would know."

"What's going on, Cam?" Justice asked, confused.

"Cam lost his girl, and she didn't even send him a text," Lyle said to Justice.

Justice sat eating his food and watched Wes and Lyle. When I looked at Justice, he frowned and shook his head.

"You think it was her parents that decided to pull her out of school?" Justice asked.

"More than likely," Wes said.

"It's always parents that make our lives miserable," Lyle said with a smirk.

"What did you do?" Wes asked.

"I didn't do anything," I said.

"You sure?" Wes asked.

"I am pretty sure," I said.

"I still don't see it," Lyle said. "I think that she was getting back at her dad or something with you."

"Yeah, that's it. That makes more sense than anything that she was trying to punish her father with you," Wes said, with an orange in his hands.

"So, you think she's transferred?" I asked.

"You know how it is here. Someone like Blue Ivy goes missing then everyone is trying to figure out where she is," Wes said. He stopped and shook his head when looking at me. "Like I said, Portia said she saw your girl this morning. Tracy said that she was transferring." Wes paused. "I just don't get how you don't know what is going on with your girl."

"Maybe she wasn't really his girl," Lyle said.

I climbed to my feet. What Wes and Lyle said was true. What they said also hurt. I turned on my heels and walked away from the lunch table and across the cafeteria to the lunchroom exit.

In the hallway I hoped to see Kyla turn the corner and be all smiles, but she did not appear. It was just me and a handful of girls in the hallway. I didn't want to talk to anyone. So, I headed to the gym. I climbed into the bleachers and sat and thought.

When I left the Hudson mansion last night Kyla gave me a hug and promised me, she would see me Friday at school. What had happened in those handful of hours to change everything?

I shook my head. I needed to clear my head.

I went to the parking lot and on the windshield of my car was an envelope. I reached out and retrieved the envelope. I opened the envelope and inside was a letter.

I read the letter. It was surprisingly short.

"Dear Cam,

"I don't always have the right words to say, but others, those who have come before me seem to know my thoughts better than me."

i carry your heart in me (i carry it in
my heart) i am never without it (anywhere
i go you go, my dear; and whatever is done
by only me is your doing, my darling)
i fear
no fate (for you are my fate, my sweet) i want
no world (for beautiful you are my world, my true)
and it's you are whatever moon has always meant
and whatever a sun will always sing is you
here is the deepest secret nobody knows
(here is the root of the root and the bud of the bud
and the sky of the sky of a tree called life; which grows
higher than soul can hope and mind can hide)
and this is the wonder that keeps the stars apart
i carry your heart (i carry it in my heart)

I smiled at the note and the poem.
I texted Kyla.
I miss you.
A few seconds later, I received a text from Kyla.
Come see me, afterschool.
I smiled. I smiled and for the first time that Friday I felt light and hopeful.